BOFFIN BRAINCHILD

BOFFIN BRAINCHILD

Jill Jennings

illustrated by
Thomas Jennings

Natterjack Books

Mary's School, Malton
dniewicz

Text copyright © Jill Jennings 2013

Text illustrations copyright © Thomas Jennings 2013

Cover illustration copyright © Russ Daff 2013

Cover design copyright © Mandy Norman 2013

Published by Natterjack Books Ltd
47 York Road, Malton, York, YO17 6AX
2013

Typeset by TW Typesetting, Plymouth, Devon
Printed and bound by CPI Group (UK) Ltd, Croydon, CR0 4YY

ISBN 978-0-9556091-1-4

British Library Cataloguing in Publication Data:
a catalogue record for this book is available from the British Library.

2 4 6 8 10 9 7 5 3 1

For Dick, Lizzie, Thomas, Pip and Alice.
Thank you for helping to bring Boffin Brainchild to life.

Chapter One

Here, at long last, was Boffin Brainchild. Tom had waited weeks for this moment. Boffin stood on a little platform in the middle of the great hall of the science museum. The white stone platform made Boffin the exact same height as Tom.

"Look! He blinks. Hey, that's cool," said Jack, pushing into Tom so hard that he fell over the rope that hung across, at waist height, to protect the robot.

"Do be careful!" shouted Mr Richardson. "Get out from there, Tom! We'll all get a chance to meet Boffin, if we take it in turns!"

Tom picked himself up from the floor and stepped back over the rope. Boffin's head moved and stared straight at him. Tom could see his own reflection upside down in the robot's eyes.

"Go on then, Thomas, say something to him! Get him to talk!" Mr Richardson raised his head again, above the excited class. He was a small man, bouncy like Granddad's terrier, Tom decided – and he yapped like it too.

Tom shrugged his shoulders. There was no way he wanted to be the first in front of the whole class, especially with Jack standing behind him, ready to jeer at whatever he said.

"Well, who is going to talk to Boffin Brainchild? He's the main reason we're here after all." Mr Richardson surveyed the group of girls and boys.

Tom flinched – Jack was poking him, sharply, in the middle of his back.

"Go on, teacher's pet! Suck up to him!"

"Oh, stop being such a jerk!" Tom whispered through gritted teeth.

"Well, if no one else will." Mr Richardson wove his way through the class, leant over the rope and said, "Hello, Boffin, my name is . . ."

Boffin Brainchild turned his head. "Oh, stop being such a jerk!" he said, in an ordinary boy's voice.

The class burst out laughing.

"Humph! That's enough. Let's leave him for now and come back a bit later." Their teacher looked at a leaflet in his hand. "If we carry on down here and turn right, we'll find the amazing acrobatic robot. Come on, keep up, everyone!"

"Mr Richardson, I don't feel well." Tom, clutching his stomach, eased himself on to a nearby bench. He knew his teacher couldn't bear the sight of anyone being sick. "Can I sit here for a while?" he asked.

"Not on your own."

"But . . ."

"You can't be left on your own, and that's final."

"There's a guard over there and look, another one down the hall."

"I'd still rather you came with us into the other room. There'll be benches in there too."

"But if I move I'll be sick." Tom hunched over till his face almost touched his knees.

He heard his teacher's intake of breath, and then felt a reassuring pat on his shoulder. "Well, if you're feeling that bad. Are you sure you'll be okay?"

Tom nodded.

"I'll stay with him, Sir!" Jack flopped down next to Tom on the bench.

"No!" said Tom, sliding away. "I want to be on my own, Sir. I need quiet."

"You're positive?"

"Yes!" cried Tom. The sound came out louder than he'd meant it to. Jack smirked.

Mr Richardson raised his eyebrows high above the rims of his round glasses. They remained suspended while he thought. Tom had to bite into his bottom lip to stop himself smiling. If only his teacher would let his eyebrows down, but the longer they stayed up there, the harder it was for Tom to stay looking sick. He tried not to think of the cartoons he'd drawn of his teacher with this very look on his face. No man should have eyebrows that went that high. They made Mr Richardson look like an owl.

Tom covered his mouth with his hand and coughed the laugh away.

The rest of the class were getting restless.

"Can we go now, Sir?" Sophie asked.

"Yes, in just a moment."

"I'll be fine," said Tom. "I don't want to stop the others seeing the rest of the robots."

Mr Richardson gave him a kindly smile. "That's thoughtful of you. Right, Jack, come on!" He turned to Tom. "We'll give you some peace and quiet for now, but I'll be back to check on you in a short while. You're not to leave this spot. All right?" His teacher stood in front of him, rustling about in his anorak pocket. He finally pulled out a crinkled paper bag. "Use this if you need to."

Tom watched his class move away. Jack was at the back, twirling a key ring round and round on his finger and walking in his I'm-so-cool way.

It would be great, Tom thought, if he tripped and fell flat on his face.

As soon as they were out of sight Tom got up, stuffed the paper bag into his backpack and stood once more in front of Boffin.

This was the moment he'd wanted for so long – ever since he'd read about the world's first free-thinking robot. All the science magazines and websites had been full of Boffin Brainchild: the robot designed to learn as a human child does, by watching and listening. This moment was too important to share with Jack.

Tom looked around. There was no one nearby. Even the guard had moved away to the other end of the long white hall and was busy talking to a woman there. Their voices echoed around the high-ceilinged room. Metal robotic birds hung down from steel rafters. Glass cases held tiny exhibits, including a moving metal centipede. At any other time, Tom would have been keen to see it, but not now. There was only one robot he wanted to see: the one standing before him.

Boffin Brainchild was just as the website had described. He had a very realistic face and natural looking hands, even down to the fingernails. The rest of his body looked mechanical, but Tom wasn't bothered about that. He was more interested in seeing how the robot worked and if it really was as clever as it was meant to be.

5

Tom let his head fall to the side. It took him a moment to realise that Boffin Brainchild had slowly moved his head to the same position. Ignoring the sign which read "Do not touch", he stretched out a finger and touched the end of Boffin's nose.

There was a gentle whirring sound. Boffin Brainchild's

hand, with forefinger out-stretched, extended itself smoothly towards Tom. He felt a warm gentle pressure on the tip of his nose.

Tom touched Boffin on the chin, Boffin reached out to Tom's chin. When Tom patted his own head, Boffin mimicked him. Tom bent forward and touched his toes. The robot bent forward, in one continuous motion, and did the same.

"You're incredible."

"Thank you," said Boffin Brainchild.

If Tom had left it at that, perhaps his life would have stayed the same as it had always been. But he needed to know exactly how Boffin worked. Were his eyes soft, or hard like mini cameras? How was the robot able to copy his exact movements? Questions buzzed through Tom's mind. He moved closer still and touched Boffin's left eye, planning to cover it, to see if that would stop Boffin working. Immediately Boffin raised a finger and poked Tom in his left eye.

"Ouch! That really hurt!"

"Hurt! Ouch! Tom felt pain. Finger in eye causes pain. Boffin sorry, did not want to hurt." He covered his own eye, like Tom was doing.

"How do you know my name? And please stop copy-ing me."

"I learn when I copy, that is how I learn." He

began to clap his hands together. "Boffin clever boy."

"Yes, yes . . . sshh!"

"Does Tom like Boffin Brainchild?"

"I think you're very clever – for a robot."

Boffin clapped again and chanted, "Boffin clever boy."

There was something out of control about the robot that made Tom back away. He was behaving like a toddler. It wasn't what Tom had expected.

"Got to go now."

"Don't. Stay!"

"I can't, the museum will be closing soon. I've got to get back to the others."

"Want to go with Tom. Not like it here in smelly museum."

Boffin Brainchild stepped off his platform, climbed over the rope and caught hold of Tom's hand.

"No! Let go!" Tom tugged his hand free. "Get back on your stand, before someone sees."

"Want to go with Tom!"

"No!"

"Yes!"

"No!" said Tom. "And keep your voice down." He looked across – the guard was facing the other way, still talking. "You're going to get me into trouble." He gave the robot a gentle push towards the stand.

"Oh, stop being such a jerk!" said Boffin.

Tom smiled – he knew where he'd learnt that from.

"Look, sorry, but I can't take you with me. You belong here. I'll come and visit you some time."

"You won't!"

"Okay, maybe not, I've got to go."

Hurrying across the white marbled floor, Tom heard rapid *chink*, *chinks* of metallic footsteps behind him. The sounds echoed around the huge hall and Tom spotted the museum guard looking in their direction.

"Go away!" Tom hissed over his shoulder. "I'm not taking you with me."

Boffin sank to his knees, then lay back on the floor and stuck his legs up in the air. He began to scream in a high-pitched voice as he threshed his arms and legs about.

"I'm not staying! I wanna go home. Wanna go home now! Wanna go home now!"

"Stop it!" Tom looked back over his shoulder. The guard was walking their way. "Okay, okay. You can come with me, but only if you stop making a fuss. Right now!"

"Boffin will be good."

"You off your perch again, Boffin? Going walkabout?" the tall guard asked.

"I didn't get him to, honest," said Tom. "He won't leave me alone."

The guard laughed. "I believe you. We put up signs everywhere to tell people not to touch him, so they don't half get a shock when he hops off his stand and latches on to them. It's how he learns, you know. Yesterday, he took a shine to a mother with two toddlers. We had to rescue the poor woman and shut him away in the office for a bit. Let us know if he gets too much, but otherwise it's okay to have him walking around. He has a security bracelet that stops him from leaving the museum."

Boffin showed Tom the bracelet.

"He's clever, isn't he?" said the guard. "He knows exactly what we're saying."

"Yes, Boffin clever boy." Clap, clap.

"Hey, Mike!" called the guard from the far hallway. "There's ructions in the other room. Some kid's gone and got himself trapped in the self-piloted car."

"Not another one. They never read the sign." He hurried off.

I bet it's Jack, Tom thought. He looked at Boffin Brainchild and wished he had told the guard that he'd had enough. The robot was watching him intently, mimicking every slight movement, even down to his blinking.

"Quit copying me! I don't like it."

"Okay, but can Boffin come home with you?"

Tom let out a long breath. *How was he going to*

10

get rid of this annoying robot? He thought fast. "Yes, okay? You can come with me. But first of all I have to find the Men's?"

"Mens gone," said Boffin, pointing to the doorway.

"No, I don't mean men, I mean . . . loos."

"What will Tom lose?"

Tom sighed. "I want to go to the toilet. Get it?"

"Boffin not able to get toilet, but toilets are down corridor, first on right. See, boss taught me that. Boffin clever boy." Clap, clap.

"Be quiet! Sshh!" Tom put his finger to his lips.

Boffin copied straightaway. "Sshh!" He let the sound out slowly, then kept repeating this action as he followed. When they reached the toilets, Tom shouldered the heavy door open and prayed that no one was in there. He bent down and checked under all the doors. No feet.

"What are those?" Boffin pointed towards a row of urinals.

"They're . . . no time to explain. In here!" He held a cubicle door open.

Boffin walked in. "What is this?"

"A toilet! Will you stop with all the questions? Stay here until I've finished. If anyone comes, stay quiet. Okay?"

"Okay."

11

"I'm going to close the door now. I'll be in the next one."

Tom shut the door on Boffin. Reaching out, he banged the next cubicle door, but instead of going in he tiptoed back out of the toilets.

The great exhibition hall was still empty. With no sign of the guards, Tom went to find his classmates and Mr Richardson. They weren't in the next room, but the tall guard he'd spoken to earlier was there.

Tom went up to him. "Er, I've just played a trick on Boffin Brainchild," he began. "He's in the toilets. He wanted me to take him home. But I can't."

The guard laughed. "Course not, son. Don't worry, he'll get over it. I'll go fetch him, but you'd better make yourself scarce. Go look at some of the exhibits in the other halls. You were clever to dodge him. He can be persistent."

"Yeah, that's for sure."

The guard chuckled, "Poor Boffin!" and shook his head at some private joke.

"If my teacher comes looking for me, will you tell him I've gone to look in the other room?"

"Excuse me, dear." An elderly woman had appeared at their side. She started asking for directions to the tea room.

"I'll show you," said the guard.

"You'll tell my teacher, won't you?" Tom called after them. The guard nodded.

Tom went through to where he thought his class was, but the self-piloted car was empty and there was no sign of them. He stopped to look at the car for a moment, but then out of the corner of his eye saw Boffin leaving the toilets. He knew the robot had seen him. There was still no sign of Mr Richardson, or of the class. Boffin was walking in his direction. *Yikes*, Tom thought. *I'm going to have to get out of here.*

He hurried away, dodging in and out of groups of people. He thought he'd lost the robot, but near the exit saw him again. It was no use. He would have to go outside. The robot couldn't follow him there. He paused in between the large double doors, to look for the distinctive red top of their bus. There it was, parked by the pavement.

Pigeons fluttered up as Tom wove his way through them. They settled again in his wake, greedily pecking at chunks of half-eaten sandwich that a small child was throwing at them. A doting dad was photographing the whole scene.

There was no sign of the bus driver, so Tom sat on the tarmac in the late afternoon sunshine. The evening rush hour was beginning and with it a constant drone of traffic, broken by squeals of brakes as the traffic

13

lights further along the road changed. Tom looked up and realised the bus door was slightly open, so he got to his feet and climbed aboard. It was hot and stuffy inside. Halfway down the aisle, he shoved his backpack into an overhead shelf and slid into a window seat.

Lying back against the plush upholstery, he closed his eyes. It had been a long day, with two and a half hours of travelling to get here. He heard someone entering the bus and their slow, heavy footfalls as they walked down the carpeted aisle towards him.

Tom opened his eyes.

It was Boffin Brainchild.

"See! Boffin did like Tom said, made sure no one saw him. Boffin clever boy!" He began to clap.

How did you . . .? You're not supposed to leave the museum. Your bracelet!"

"I took it off. See!" Boffin showed his bare wrist.

"But how did you find me?"

"Boffin saw you on the security cameras, before disabling them. See Boffin did as Tom said. No one saw Boffin."

Tom's mouth dropped open. He quickly shut it, banging his top and bottom teeth together.

"You've got to get out of here. Now! Go back to the museum!" Tom felt his heart begin to race. "Go on, get out! Get off the bus now!"

"But Tom said yes to Boffin. Boffin asked to go home with Tom, and Tom said yes."

"Don't you understand? You're going to get me into trouble. You've got to go back, before . . . oh no, too late! Quick, get in here! Down!"

Tom pulled Boffin into the seat beside him and then pushed him flat on the floor. He'd seen Mr Richardson leading the class into the car park.

"Squeeze under the seat. Quick! Boffin, please . . . hurry!"

Jack was first on the bus.

"Well, where is poooor Tom? Where ya hiding? Jacky Wacky wants to make sure you're all better now."

Boffin was most of the way under the seat, but his head and shoulders wouldn't fit. Tom jumped up and got his bag from the shelf, dropping it on Boffin's head just as Jack threw himself on the seat next to him.

"What you playing at?"

Tom felt his face colour. Had Jack seen?

"You're in big trouble. Mr Richardson was looking everywhere for you. It's your fault we didn't get long enough in the shop." Jack caught hold of Tom's cheek and pinched it hard. "Getting a bit of colour back in your cheeks, I see."

"Let go, Jack!"

"Make me!"

"Let go, Jack!" said a voice from near Tom's feet.

Jack was too busy turning the pinch of flesh to notice.

"Go on, beg," said Jack.

The seats were filling up around them, but nobody seemed to take any notice. Jack suddenly let go; Mr Richardson was walking down the bus.

"Jack! Out of there! Leave Tom alone."

"But I want to sit here, Sir."

"You can sit beside me. Get a move on, the bus is about to go!"

Tom's teacher leant forward and put his hand on the empty seat beside Tom. His eyes, magnified by the thick lenses of his glasses, had no warmth in them. Tom swallowed.

"I'm disappointed, Thomas." Tom could smell peppermint on his teacher's breath as he spoke. "I trusted you to do as you were told. You shouldn't have left the museum."

"I didn't mean to, Sir. I told the guard . . ."

"Yes, I finally met up with him, but only after getting extremely worried about not being able to find you. He told me you were in Hall B, but you weren't. I searched everywhere. It meant that the entire class missed out on seeing Boffin Brainchild again."

"I'm sorry, Sir."

"I'm sure you are. Think before you act next time.

Well, how are you feeling? Still not right I see. Judging by that red cheek, I'd say you have a temperature."

"I'm okay." Tom attempted a small smile.

"Well, I hope we make it home without any further problems." Mr Richardson nodded curtly and walked back up the aisle, barking orders at the class as he passed. "Do that seat belt up! And sit down, Em!"

Tom slipped off his jacket and draped it over the bag at his feet. His heart was thumping so fast, he could hear it drumming in his ears. How come both Jack and Mr Richardson had failed to see Boffin? He felt the weight of the robot's head resting on his foot. Looking down, he was relieved to see that the bag was doing a good job of hiding Boffin.

The girls in the seat across the aisle were texting away on their mobiles, showing them to each other. They kept smiling over at Tom. Thankfully the coach seats had tall backs, so he was cocooned from the pupils in front and behind him.

I wish those girls would stop looking at me.

Tom glared back, which seemed to do the trick, but then they started giggling. He ignored them and stared out of the window. Finally, they got up and moved further up the coach, to sit near their friends. He heard a burst of girly chatter.

The bus lurched into motion. They were off at last.

Tom bent down and lifted a sleeve of his jacket. The pupils in Boffin's eyes dilated as the light hit them.

"Boffin being good and quiet."

"No, no! Don't clap. If anyone sees you, I'll get into big trouble and they'll take you straight back to the museum."

"Boffin wants to stay with Tom."

"Looks like you're going to have to. Be very still and don't speak till I tell you. Okay?"

Boffin nodded his head. "Oops, Boffin moved."

"Hey, Tom!" A blond haired boy's face appeared in front of him, squashed thin in the narrow gap between the seats.

"Yeah, Phil, what do you want?"

"Why are you talking to yourself? And could you stop kicking my seat?"

"Sorry. I'll try not to."

Phil pulled his face out of the gap. Seconds later it popped up over the back of his seat. "Do you know where Boffin Brainchild went?"

"Why should I?" Tom felt his cheeks getting hot. He wished Phil would turn around, sit down and shut up.

"Well, when we'd all gone back to see him, he'd disappeared. Mr Richardson wasn't happy, not after we'd gone to the museum specially to see 'The world's first

18

free-thinking robot'. Do you think he really does have proper feelings, like you and me?"

"Philip, will you turn around and put your seatbelt back on? Sit properly," bellowed Mr Richardson from the front of the bus. "And that goes for you lot. The back seat isn't a playing field. Put that ball down. Now!"

Mr Richardson sent his extra hard stare around the entire bus, his eyes owl-like again. Then in a deep voice he said, "If you'd all behaved properly, instead of mucking about in the self-piloted car, we might have been able to see Boffin Brainchild again. Let that be a lesson to you all. It pays to listen to your teacher! *Put the ball down, Harry!*"

Chapter Two

The journey had taken ages. All that time Tom had to sit with his secret by his feet, terrified that Boffin would jump up and do something. He felt so tense that all the muscles along his shoulders and across the back of his neck began to ache. And then he started to really feel sick. He felt every sway of the bus and every bump on the road. Tom had never felt so scared in his life. But Boffin remained totally quiet and still.

Tom, recognising a petrol station, bent forward and whispered, "We're nearly there, Boffin. No, don't move yet. Sshh! You'll hear everyone else getting up, but stay still. Don't make a sound. We need everyone to get off the bus first."

The coach drove in through the school gates, gave a wide turn and came to a stop by a short flight of steps.

With a great surge of chattering, everyone jumped up. Everyone except for Tom. He slumped lower in his seat and pretended to be asleep.

"Tom, wake up! We're here!" It was Phil. Tom ignored

him, squeezing his eyes tighter and waiting for the movement of students to stop and the sound of voices to hush. Then, opening his eyes, he pulled himself up slowly so that he could look over the seat in front.

"You all right, Tom?" Mr Richardson was still on the bus and heading his way.

Tom dropped back into his seat.

"Not really," he said, as his teacher stood over him. "I tried to get up, but I got a horrible feeling here!" Tom pointed to his side. "I can't move. Aagh!" Tom cried. "Think I'm going to be sick!"

"Stay still. I'll go get help . . ." Mr Richardson's face was full of concern. He spun around and walked quickly back up the bus aisle.

Tom felt mean.

"Keep an eye on him, will you?" Mr Richardson fired his words at the driver as he climbed down from the bus. "He's feeling nauseous. I'll fetch someone to help."

"Well, I don't want him getting sick all over my bus."

"Someone will be back as quickly as possible," Mr Richardson barked.

Tom peeped up and watched him hurry away over the tarmac.

The driver came down the bus, his pink-shirted pot belly arriving first. "Now then, young lad, might be best if you get off the bus and fill those lungs of yours with fresh air. Nothing like it for making you feel better. Up you get!"

Tom pretended to try, but then doubled over. "Oh, the pain! It's terrible. Please get Mr Richardson! Quick! Ahhh!"

The driver's chins wobbled as he nodded. "I'll go fetch him straight away. Hold tight!"

Tom waited until the driver had disappeared through the school's main entrance. There was no one else about.

"Quick, Boffin, they've all gone. Come out of there!"

Tom kept a lookout as the robot eased himself up by his front arms.

"Hurry up!" Tom said.

"Boffin can't. Foot stuck."

"In what?" Tom dropped down to his knees on the dusty floor and looked under the seat. Boffin's right foot was wedged between it and the bus wall. Tom reached in and tugged at the leg. It wouldn't budge. "Twist your foot around!"

"Twist? What is twist?"

"Why is everything so difficult with you? This – look!" Tom lay back on the floor and rotated his right

22

foot. Boffin watched, copied the motion and his foot came free.

"Great, now come on, quickly, before they come back." Tom grabbed his jacket and bag. "Hurry!" He gave Boffin a gentle push.

"Oh, stop being such a jerk!"

"Hey, I'm not being a jerk. I'm just trying to help you. You're the one that's got us into this mess. Stay here if you want to. I'm going." He squeezed past Boffin and marched up the aisle and off the bus.

"Wait!" The robot hurried after him. "Sorry. No, Boffin not sorry. What did Boffin do wrong?"

"Oh, great! They're coming! Now what? Here, under the bush! Down, Boffin, and be quiet!"

Tom stood in front of the evergreen shrub, hoping they wouldn't see past him.

"So you've got off the bus then. Good lad!" the bus driver smiled at Tom, then looked anxiously at Mr Richardson. "He was doubled right over. I wouldn't have fetched you otherwise. It's his appendix, that's what it is. A bad pain like that." The driver climbed back on the bus.

"You'd better come in and sit down, Tom. I'll phone your parents. See if they can come and fetch you."

"No, don't call them! I . . . I'm much better now.

They're expecting me to walk home, as usual. Like the driver said, the fresh air really helped."

"You do look better." Mr Richardson's shoulders dropped with relief. "Has the pain gone?"

Tom nodded.

"I expect it's just travel sickness. Often happens on long coach journeys. You'll probably be fine now. But I want you to tell your parents about the pain."

Tom nodded again. He heard a rustle in the bush and hoped Mr Richardson hadn't noticed.

"Well, so long as you're all right now." He thanked the bus driver before hurrying off.

"Right, young lad, have you got all your stuff off the bus?" the driver called from his seat. "Cos I'd like to be getting on my way now too."

Tom gave a thumbs-up sign. *Just go*, he thought.

Three long blasts from the bus horn, a big salute from the driver and the coach pulled away from the kerb. Tom waited for the tail lights to disappear through the gates then, making sure no one was watching, he ducked into a tight space between the bush and the wall behind it.

"Boffin, where are you?"

"Here! Boffin dirty. Dirt on Boffin's hands. Look!"

"Don't worry, it's only soil. Let's go!"

Boffin crawled from under the bush and stood up in the narrow gap between it and the wall. Tom looked the robot up and down. Everything that afternoon had happened in a rush. He'd constantly been hiding Boffin behind or under something. In some strange way, because of the robot's realistic face and hands, Tom had forgotten about the rest of his body. But there was no way he was going to get Boffin down the street without drawing serious attention.

Below Boffin's boyish face and neck was a hard plastic chest, which hinted at ribs underneath. Then there was a round plastic plate with an absurd tummy button in the middle. Each of Boffin's arms was in four rigid parts: the shoulder and upper arm, a small elbow joint, the lower arm – with a complicated wrist joint – and finally, at the end, a perfectly realistic hand. The hands were the same size as Tom's.

Boffin's legs were made up of hard plastic thighs, complicated kneecaps and shin-plates. Some plastic coated wires were just visible at the ankle, above his metal feet. Each foot had five silver toes, jointed like a human's.

"I think you'd better wear this." Tom held out his jacket.

Boffin held it between thumb and forefinger and looked straight at Tom.

"Try it on!" Tom urged.

"Try it on, what?"

"Oh, here, give it to me. Look! I want you to do this!" Tom went through the motions of donning the jacket. "See?"

Boffin was soon putting it on, just as Tom had done. But after a couple of seconds he began tugging it off again.

"No, keep it on. You've got to wear it. It makes you look normal and, er . . . clever."

Boffin clapped.

"What's with the clapping? You're not a toddler. Stop it and hold your hands out!"

Tom zipped the jacket closed, under Boffin's chin. "I don't know what we're going to do about your legs." He tilted his head to one side. Boffin did too, jerking up straight again when Tom clicked his fingers.

"My PE kit! It's in my locker. Go hide under the bush again while I get it. What are you doing now?"

Boffin was looking intently at his thumb and forefinger and brushing one against the other.

"Why can't Boffin make noise with his fingers, like Tom?"

"Quit messing! We haven't got time for it. Hide!"

Boffin scrambled on his hands and knees under the bush.

"Don't come out till I tell you to, okay?"

*   *   *

The locker room was quiet. Tom could hear a distant droning from the assembly hall. His heart hammered as he raced from the building and back down to the shrubbery. Checking that no one had seen, he squeezed in behind the bush.

"Look what I've got for you." He held out a navy tracksuit bottom and a pair of trainers.

Boffin didn't respond. All Tom could see were two bright blue eyes staring out.

"Are you coming out or what?"

"Tom hasn't said to."

"Come out!" he said impatiently. "And put these on!" He handed over the tracksuit trousers.

Boffin held them in outstretched arms for a moment, then tried pushing his hand into one of the legs.

"No, it's not a jacket."

Snatching them back, Tom pulled them on over his jeans. "See?" He wriggled out of them and threw the trousers back at Boffin. "Be quick!"

Boffin's body whirred as it went through the complicated motions. "Boffin clever boy," he said, once they were on. Clap, clap.

Tom raised his eyes skywards. "Now the trainers – sit down and put your feet straight out."

Slipping the shoes on each foot, Tom drew the laces together on one and tied a bow. Boffin, hardly blinking, watched closely.

"Right, now the other foot," said Tom.

"No!" Boffin stilled Tom's hand and lifted it away. "Boffin shut shoe now."

Tom shook his head. "We're in a hurry. I will."

"Boffin do it."

"No!" Tom crossed the laces, but Boffin jiggled and pulled his foot free. Tom ignored him and caught up the lace again. Boffin kicked out, narrowly missing Tom's kneecap.

"Boffin do it! Boffin do it!"

"You crazy robot! Quit it or I'll leave you here on your own." Tom meant it. He was tired, hungry and hunched over in a hedge. He didn't want any of this. Boffin stopped wriggling. Tom looked into a pair of very human eyes that were wide with shock.

"Sorry," said the robot. "Boffin sorry."

"Forget it. Come on, get up."

Boffin did, but then toppled forward. Tom put out his hand. *Thwack!* It collided with a very hard chest.

"Watch out. That hurt!"

"Boffin can't walk in trainers. Need to feel ground with sensors in toes."

"You've got to wear them. No one must see your metal feet."

"Tom not like Boffin's feet?"

"Oh, don't be stupid."

"Boffin not stupid! Boffin most intelligent robot ever made. First proper free-thinking robot, designed by the world's leading robotics engineers, Ishi Kashikoi and Felicity Brown."

"Just stop talking, will you? You wanted to come home with me, I didn't ask you to. This is not home and it isn't safe. Someone could spot us any minute." He poked his head out through the bush.

Boffin copied. Tom drew his head back, not realising the robot was behind him. Their heads collided.

"Ouch! Look, let's start again. Could you be a . . . a clever boy – which you are of course – and could you try very hard to take a few steps in your clever new shoes?"

"Yes, Tom."

Boffin took a step and wobbled. Then another one and wobbled again. "Can Boffin hold Tom's hand?"

"No." He picked up his bag and slung it over his shoulder. "Hang on! We've forgotten your head."

"My head? Where is it? Where's Boffin's head gone?" Boffin reached up with his hands.

Tom laughed. "It's okay. It's still there. I meant you're bald. No hair. See! You don't have this." Tom lifted up a strand of hair from the top of his head. Boffin copied the movement, but no hair came up with his fingers.

"Boffin not boy then, not same as Tom."

"Hey, don't worry about that. All boys are different."

"How?"

"I'll tell you later." Tom put his bag down, unzipped it and felt around for his navy baseball cap.

"You can wear this, but I'll want it back later." He pulled the hat down over Boffin's head and nodded approval. "Looks okay to me. You'll pass for a normal boy now."

"Really? Thank you."

"That's all right." Tom turned, stepped out from behind the bush and waited for Boffin to follow. The robot staggered out, then wobbled violently as he tried to walk along the pavement. As they reached the kerb, Tom put his hand out to steady him. Boffin grasped it.

"Why would people put spots on us?"

"What? What are you talking about now?"

Boffin managed the shallow step down, but then stopped halfway across the road. "When we were hiding in the bush, Tom said he was scared someone was going to spot us."

"You can't stand in the middle of the road." Tom tugged at the robot's hand, but he wouldn't budge. "There's a car coming! Someone's going to spot you right now."

"Don't want spots."

Boffin, still holding Tom's hand, broke into a chaotic run and pulled Tom after him – straight into the path of the oncoming car. Just in time, it swerved around them. Tom caught a glimpse of who was sitting in the passenger seat. Jack! His dad hit the car horn and the angry sound blared all the way up the street.

Great, thought Tom. *It just had to be Jack, didn't it?* He sighed as he pulled Boffin up the kerb. *He'll give me hell tomorrow at school. That's if I can go at all, with this robot to look after.*

Chapter Three

Tom knew that Mum and Dad wouldn't be home for another half hour, which might give him time to settle Boffin into his bedroom. The trouble was, how was he going to get the robot up the stairs? Boffin was so excited at being in a real home that he wanted to know what everything was and what it was used for.

"Table. I know what a table is, that was what I started life on. That is a ch . . ." Boffin froze.

"What's up? Speak to me! Boffin!"

The only sound in the room was a strange whirring, coming from deep inside the robot's chest.

". . . air," said Boffin.

"You need some air? But, hang on, you don't breathe."

"I said ch . . . air. Does Tom have a mummy and daddy?"

"Yes. They're going to be home soon. What am I going to say to them? Hey, Mum! Dad! You know I went to the museum to see the famous robot, well, ta-da! Here he is! I don't think so. Going to have to think of something fast." Tom shook his head, looked up and saw Boffin copying him. "They're going to kill me!"

"No!" Boffin screwed up his face. "That's wrong. Killing is wrong! Against human law! Guts spilled! Squiggly, yucky things!"

"Sshh, sshh! It's okay. Boffin, it's okay. I didn't mean it. They wouldn't kill me, no matter what. I just meant they'll be cross with me."

"Cross?"

"Angry. Do you know what that means?"

"Yes, Ishi says it means feeling or showing annoyance."

"There you go then, cross means the same thing. Look, when Mum and Dad get in, let me do the talking, okay? And please try not to clap – and don't say 'Boffin is a clever boy'."

"Tom gives lots of orders. Boffin can think for himself, is world's first free-thinking robot and likes to talk to people, that is how to learn new things. Boffin clever at . . ." He'd frozen again and was making a strange sucking noise, but his mouth wasn't moving. The sound seemed to come from behind him. Tom looked, and saw a round patch at the top of Boffin's trousers being sucked inwards. Then a horrible high-pitched whining sound developed, like a vacuum cleaner trying to suck up a loose rug.

"What's happening?" Tom asked, but Boffin was well and truly frozen. The noise was deafening. Tom had to stop it. He caught hold of the tracksuit bottom and pulled it away. The noise stopped immediately and Boffin finished his sentence, ". . . learning new things."

"Hang on!" Tom said. "Before you start looking at something else, I need to make sure you're all right. You weren't working properly. But you should be okay now. I uncovered that." Tom showed Boffin. "I think it's an air vent. There!" He pointed at a tiny silver grid.

"FART," said Boffin.

"What?"

"FART." The robot put his hands on his hips. "Forced Air Refrigeration Technovalve, designed by Ishi Kashikoi and Felicity Brown. It is very good for me to have FART. It makes sure that Boffin doesn't get too hot. That's what Ishi Kashikoi and Felicity Brown told me. They were very happy when Boffin's FART worked for the first time. They laughed and laughed."

"I bet. Ha ha! Very clever of them! But I don't think you should call it your fart any more. I think Dr Ishi was making fun of you."

"Fun of me! What does that mean?"

"Tell you later. Do you want to see upstairs or not?"

"Yes."

"Better hurry then. Follow me."

34

Tom bounded up the stairs, as he usually did. When he reached the landing he looked down to see how Boffin was managing. The robot was about a quarter of the way up.

"Well done," said Tom and immediately wished he hadn't, because Boffin looked up, lost his footing and stumbled backwards. For a second he resembled a starfish, his arms and legs outstretched, before he fell flat on his back at the foot of the stairs.

"Boffin!" Tom went running down. "You okay?"

"No. Stupid, stupid shoes! Can I take them off now?"

"Yeah, think you'd better. I'll help you. Watch closely. Then you'll be able to put them on and off by yourself."

"Boffin would like that. Boffin thinks Tom is nice."

"Don't get mushy, Boffin. Boys don't get mushy with each other. People will think you're soft and pick on you. So you have to be a bit tough when you're a boy." Tom pulled the trainers off. "Go on, you go up first. I'll carry these for you."

Tom followed closely, with hands at the ready just in case. Without the shoes, Boffin managed the stairs easily. Tom saw how his legs and ankle joints had to adjust to each step.

"You're incredible," he said when they got to the top. "I've never seen such a smooth-moving robot before. I knew you were special. That's why I couldn't wait to see you at the museum."

"Don't get mushy, Tom. Boys don't get mushy with each other."

Tom smiled. "That door on the left is Mum's and Dad's bedroom. Next is the bathroom. Then that's the spare bedroom, and this one's mine." He pushed the door inwards.

"Small room," said Boffin.

"It's not," said Tom. "It's a normal-sized bedroom."

"Is it?"

"Yes. Watch out! You're treading on my drawings. Move!"

Tom pulled a page out from under Boffin's feet. "Nah! It's rubbish anyway." He scrunched it up and threw it into a wastepaper basket in the corner.

"Clever Tom!" said Boffin. "Good shot!"

Tom smiled.

"Boffin help Tom." He bent over and picked up a piece of paper, scrunched it tightly in his fist and threw.

"No!" cried Tom. "That was a good picture. I wanted to keep that one for my comic."

"Whoops, sorry," said Boffin, retrieving a paper ball from the bin. He opened out the crumpled sheet and looked at it.

"Good drawing of robot."

"That's the picture I dumped," said Tom.

"Why?"

"Because it's not good enough for my comic."

"Comic? Does Tom make his own comic?"

"Yeah. It's fun."

"Please can Boffin look at it? Boffin likes comics."

"You read? I haven't shown my stuff to anyone before, but if you want to look at one, they're all in here."

Tom opened his bedside cupboard and pulled out an armful. He dropped them on his bed. "This is the one I'm working on now, called 'Robot Zone'. If you want, you can look at it later. But I'll show you around the room first. This is my bed. I'll get the fold-up one from the guest room for you."

"Boffin is going to have his own bed?"

"Sure. Well, that's if you want to?"

"Yes. Boffin wants to, very much. Ishi Kashikoi used to sleep on bed in lab, while Boffin stood in corner."

"You can stand by the wall if you want."

"No! Boffin wants bed, like Tom's."

"I'll go and get it then."

Tom knew the bed was in the back of a built-in wardrobe. What he didn't know was that he would have to move Mum's dresses, Dad's jackets and a couple of bin bags full of clothes before he could get at it. One of the

37

bags tore as he hauled it out. It was full of clothes that he'd outgrown.

He took them back to the bedroom. "Look what I've found," he said as he hauled the bin bag through the doorway, but he dropped it when he saw what Boffin was doing.

"Careful! You shouldn't be touching that! It's delicate." He held out his hand for the small plastic model of a Moonwalker robot. "It's not finished. Can't get the front arm to work properly."

Boffin turned it over.

"No, don't do that!" Tom gently took it from him and placed it back with others on the shelf. "It was the first kit I was given. I was only seven. It doesn't do a lot. None of them can do one-millionth of what you can."

"Tom getting mushy again. Boys don't get mushy."

Tom laughed. "Come and help me with the bed. That's if you're strong enough?"

Boffin raised his right arm like a bodybuilder would when showing off his muscles. Only he didn't have any, just the hard plastic upper arm plate. "Boffin very strong. See!"

"Nah, you're just as weedy as me." Tom looked at his watch. "Uh-oh, Mum and Dad will be home any minute." He rushed to the window and looked down. No sign of their car. "What am I going to say to them?"

He paced around the room. Boffin followed him.

"Think, think, think!" Tom hit himself on the head.

"Think, think, think," said Boffin.

"Maybe it would be better if you were out in the garden when they come home. I've got my own hide-out. It's the garden shed really, but you can go in if you want to. And wait there until I call you. That way it would give me time to soften them up. I really hope they let you stay. We'd better hurry, follow me! Bring those, bring those!" Tom pointed to Boffin's trainers.

"Don't want to wear shoes. They're yucky!"

"Give them to me. Quick!" Tom held out his hands. "You can go downstairs without them. Okay? But you'll have to have to put them on before Mum and Dad see you."

Boffin nodded his head and started to clap. "Boffin can't wait to meet Mum and Dad."

Tom caught hold of Boffin's hands and held them tight together. "Listen! You've got to stop clapping every time you think you've been clever. It's babyish. Big boys don't clap like that. It's silly."

"Boffin not SILLY! Boffin very clever, first free-thinking r—"

"Shut up!"

"Shut up? How can Boffin shut up? Boffin isn't a door. Boffin isn't a box, Boffin—"

"Boffin is – driving Tom insane!"

"Boffin can't drive and doesn't know where Sane is."

Tom felt like shouting at him. Instead he stared into his bright blue eyes. It didn't do any good – Boffin stared right back. It was Tom who had to look away first.

"Follow me!" he said and they went downstairs slowly. Once at the bottom Tom turned down the hall, towards the back door. Boffin's feet chinked along the quarry tiles after him.

"See, that's why you need shoes, Boffin. Can't you hear the noise your feet are making?"

"Boffin hears. Has excellent audio quality. Felicity Brown says I can hear bat calls. Now, I can hear noise outside house. Car stopping, two doors slamming."

"They're home!" cried Tom. "Quick, out of here!"

Chapter Four

"We're lucky it wasn't them, just the neighbours," said Tom as he rushed across the lawn, "but Mum and Dad will be home any minute."

"Grass!" cried Boffin. "Squishy, squashy, like carpet." Boffin wriggled his metal toes.

Tom, stretching up on tiptoe, checked over the fence into next door's garden. There was no one about. He turned back to Boffin and smiled as the robot padded his feet up and down and brushed the green blades with the soles of his feet.

"Can you really feel with your metal feet?"

"Boffin has seventy-eight sensor pads in feet. First in world with these sensors. Boffin very clever."

Tom held his breath, waiting to see if he would clap. The robot raised his hands to, but paused with them centimetres apart. He looked at one and then the other, shook his head and let them fall back to his sides.

"Yeah!" said Tom. "Well done for not clapping. Now you're a clever robot!"

Boffin jumped up and down instead.

"Don't do that either, too babyish!"

"Aww," said Boffin, his mouth turning down. Tom saw the robot's eyes drift their gaze and fix intently on something behind him.

He spun around, afraid that his parents must have appeared, but there was nothing there except for the tall wooden fence with a flower border at its base. Boffin brushed past.

"What are you doing?"

The robot bent forward and pulled at something. He held it aloft.

"Flower!" he said, squashing it against his nose, then dropping it on the ground.

"Big deal," said Tom. "You'd better wipe your nose. You've got yellow pollen on the end of it. Wait, can you smell things as well?"

"Smell. What is smell?"

"It's what you were trying to do when you held the flower to your nose. Isn't it?"

Boffin shrugged his shoulders. "That's what girls do in picture books. Hold flowers to their noses."

"I see."

"Boffin sees very well too, but what is smell?"

"Like we've got time for this right now. 'Smell' is when you breathe something in through your nose, and you can . . . well . . . smell it . . . I don't know how to explain. I think there are kind of, like, little nerve ends in your nose that can pick up stuff in the air and tell what it's made from."

"Boffin still doesn't know what smell is."

"Tom doesn't either. It's just something I've always done."

"So nose is needed to smell things." Boffin touched the tip of his nose.

"Yeah and, if you were human, to breathe through."

Tom gently caught hold of Boffin's arm and guided him to the small wooden shed in the corner of the garden.

He pulled back a rusty bolt on the door. "Now don't ask any more questions. I want you to hide in here for now." With a whine from its hinges, the door swung open. Tom stood back to allow Boffin through.

"There's a chair in the corner. Sit, if you want to. You've got to stay out here, in the garden, until I come and get you. Do you understand? Remember – let me do all the talking with Mum and Dad. Otherwise they'll suss right away that you're not normal. And it would be straight back to the museum for you."

"Boffin doesn't want to go back. Wants to stay with Tom."

"Yeah, well, behave! Do what I say and we might be okay."

"Boffin hears another car!"

"They're here!" Tom felt his heart race. He held up his hands to Boffin. "Stay in the shed. Oh and put your trainers on!" He flung them at Boffin's feet before closing the door, then ran up the garden path into the house. With every step he was thinking, *What am I going to tell them? What?*

Dad was hanging his coat on the hook by the front door.

"Sorry we're late. The traffic was bad on the ring road. Bumper to bumper. How did the outing go? Good, was it?"

"Yeah, brilliant."

"Hi, Tom," Mum came padding downstairs in her slippers.

"That was fast," said Dad.

"Oh, I couldn't wait to get out of my office shoes. Now do we go for an easy option tonight – takeaway? What do you fancy, Tom?"

"Why don't I cook some pasta?" asked Dad. "You look tired this evening. I could have a meal ready in twenty minutes. Pasta okay with you, Tom?"

"Yeah, that would be great!"

"Right then, three of my Bella Pastas coming up. Rapido!"

Tom rolled his eyes at Dad's fake Italian accent and followed his parents through to the kitchen.

Mum bent to get something out of the fridge. She started talking, her voice muffled. "Tell us all about your trip, Tom. Was it as good as you'd expected?"

"It was okay." Tom, hovering by the sink, picked up a washing-up brush and swirled it round and round in a basin of cold washing-up water. A whirlpool developed in the middle as the made-up reasons why Boffin had come home with him went round and round in his head.

"Well, go on, give us some details," said Dad. "And move out of the way, I need to fill this up."

Tom jumped as Dad shoved a saucepan in front of him.

"Mum, Dad, there's something I need to talk to you about."

"What is it?" Mum

paused by the kitchen table, her hands full of lettuce and tomatoes. An anxious look swept over her face and creased her forehead.

Tom felt her eyes bore right into his secret. He turned to Dad instead, who was busy chopping up an onion.

"I've got a big favour to ask."

"Go on, spit it out!" Dad wiped his eyes with the back of his hand. "These onions are strong."

"Is it okay if a friend from school comes to stay?"

"You've finally made a friend? That's great, Tom," said Mum, relief showing all over her face.

"Thanks, Mum!"

"Don't get offended," said Dad. He stopped chopping the onion and put the sharp knife down. "We both know how hard you've been finding it, settling into a new school. That's all. It can be tough joining in at your age. The other kids are already set in their own groups and can be funny with strangers. It takes time, that's all. And of course you can have a friend to stay. Any time you like."

"That's great. I'll go and tell him."

"Hang on! Do you mean that he's here? Now?"

"Yeah. That's okay. Isn't it?"

Dad looked at Mum and shook his head. "It's very short notice, Tom!"

"I know. Sorry. I would have let you know if I could have, but I couldn't."

"What do you mean, *couldn't*?" asked Mum.

"It happened so quickly. He needed a place to stay and I said he could come here. Didn't think you'd mind."

"I still don't understand," said Mum. "Why did he 'need' a place to stay?"

"His parents were . . . they have a sick relation. They had to leave suddenly. Gone to the hospital. I said he could come home with me. They were happy about that. Really grateful."

"But they don't know us!" said Dad. "I wouldn't let you go and stay with complete strangers."

"They're different. More relaxed."

"*Pff!*" Mum puffed air out through pursed lips.

Dad scraped the onions off the chopping board into the hot frying pan. They sizzled straightaway. He stirred them around with a wooden spoon, releasing an aroma that made Tom's mouth water.

"Well, where is he?" said Mum as she spooned the salad into a bowl.

"I . . . I'll go and get him in a minute. Um . . . there's just one other thing."

"What?" both his parents said at the same time.

"He doesn't speak very good English. He hasn't been in the country long."

47

Dad sighed. "Great! So with no warning at all, we find ourselves caring for some child we have never met before, and one that we won't even be able to communicate with. That's brilliant, that is! His parents have a lot of nerve!"

"Sorry," said Tom.

"Well, what's done is done. You were just trying to be kind and we can hardly turn him out now." Dad stirred the onions energetically.

"No, of course not," said Mum. "Where is he? Upstairs in your room?"

"No, he's in the hideout." Seconds later Tom wished he hadn't said that, because Mum and Dad went to the window.

"What on earth is he playing at?" said Dad.

"My lovely flowers! Look at them!" cried Mum.

Tom squeezed between his parents and saw Boffin standing in the middle of Mum's flower border. He had a pink flower stuck to the end of his nose and all around his feet lay trampled yellow, pink and white flower heads.

Chapter Five

Tom rushed into the garden. "Get off the flowerbed! You've ruined it!"

He turned around – his mother's face was still pressed up to the kitchen window. "How could you be so stupid? And take that flower off the end of your nose!"

"Boffin not stupid."

"Don't start that again! You said you were going to be good for me."

"Yes, Boffin put on shoes, like Tom said."

"But you didn't stay in the shed!"

"Tom didn't say to stay in shed."

"Didn't he? Didn't I? Oh, never mind. Come here!"

Boffin stepped sideways off the border, pulling the flower off his nose as he came. He held it out as an offering. Tom knocked it out of his hand.

"No, Boffin! You were a bad, bad robot for picking all the flower heads off." Boffin's eyes widened. Tom couldn't hold their gaze. He looked down instead, to where the flower had fallen at Boffin's feet – feet that were encased in perfectly laced up trainers.

"Hey, well done for tying up your laces."

"Boffin clever boy?"

"Sort of, but I'm still cross with you. Mum loves her flowers and you tore all their heads off. Why did you do it?"

"Boffin was trying to smell . . ."

"Look! Mum's waving us in. Go on, wave back. That's enough, Boffin, you're not a bird. Stop waving! You're looking silly again."

"Boffin not silly. Don't like being called silly. Boffin learning to be most clever robot in world."

"Yeah, well you're not there yet. Sorry! Look, they're waiting for us. We've got to go in."

Tom saw the robot safely to the foot of the stairs. "Quick! Go to my bedroom. I'll be up in a minute."

"Tom!" Dad called sharply. Tom hardly ever heard his dad use that tone.

He went through to the kitchen.

"He's really sorry. It was an accident."

"An accident? What on earth happened?" asked Dad.

"Didn't look like an accident to me," said Mum. "Looked like he'd done it deliberately. Why would he do something like that? It was pure vandalism!"

"It wasn't all his fault. I'm to blame too. We were playing football and . . . he's useless."

"You're telling me," said Dad.

"It was me who kicked the ball. He tried to stop it from going over into next door's garden, but missed it and went flying backwards into the bed."

Tom saw Mum's forehead crease in doubt, but then it smoothed out again.

"Well, you'd better go and get your ball back. Just hope it hasn't gone into their greenhouse."

"No, I'm sure it didn't."

"Where is he now?"

"Gone upstairs. He feels embarrassed."

"I suppose accidents happen," Mum said. "Tell him not to worry about the flowers, will you? Tell him he can come down and no one will get cross with him."

Tom suddenly felt terrible for lying.

"And the pasta will be ready in five minutes." Dad tasted a piece from the saucepan. "Yep, nearly cooked. Make sure you're both down in time."

A sudden loud crashing sound came from the hall.

Tom went rushing out to find Boffin flat on his back with his legs in the air.

"Oh, Bof—"

"Are you all right?" Dad appeared, followed closely by Mum.

"Oh dear," she cried. "You haven't broken anything, have you? Here, let me have a look." She tried pushing past Tom, but he wouldn't move.

"He's fine," he said, holding his arms out so they couldn't get near. "Don't fuss!" Tom bent forward, caught hold of Boffin's hands and hauled him upright.

"Can you move your limbs all right?" asked Mum.

Boffin stared at her and sucked in his lips.

"He's okay. I'll just help him upstairs."

"No, Tom. Let him stay down here for a few minutes. That was a nasty fall. If he can walk, bring him through to the living room. He can rest there. I'll get some extra cushions." Mum scurried away.

Dad held the door open and pointed to the settee.

"Come on," Tom whispered. "But no talking, Boffin, okay? You're not to say a word!"

Boffin nodded.

"Here, sit back!" Mum plumped up a cushion and placed it behind Boffin's back. She gently touched the robot's hand. Tom held his breath. Would she notice that it wasn't a human one?

52

"Are you all right?" she asked.

Tom blurted out, "He's not *all* right, he's half left."

Mum and Dad exchanged glances.

"Joke, get it?" said Tom, desperate for Mum to back away from Boffin.

"Joke," said Boffin, and laughed heartily. There was something deeply infectious about the sound. It was  the first time Tom had heard him laugh and, probably from nerves, he found himself laughing too.

"We'll go and finish making supper," said Dad, smiling. "Do you like pasta? What is your name? Tom hasn't told us yet."

Boffin stopped laughing immediately. So did Tom. Boffin stared at Dad. Dad waited.

"Finn!" said Tom. "His name's Finn."

"Finn. Isn't that Irish?" Mum asked.

"Might be, but he's spent most of his life in Japan," Tom said.

"How exciting." Dad let out a low whistle. "I've always wanted to go there. Would give anything to see the Bullet Train."

"Dad!" Tom cried. "Is that the pasta boiling over?" His father rushed out.

"I'd better go and finish the salad," Mum smiled.

As soon as they were alone, Tom said, "You did very well. I know it was hard, but thanks for not talking. Well apart from saying 'Joke' that is. And I hadn't thought about it, but we can't use your real name here. It'll have to be Finn from now on."

"Bof-fin."

"No! Not Boffin. Just Finn."

"No! Boffin."

"Sshh, Mum's coming back!"

"I thought you'd both like a drink." She held out a small tray. "Some orange juice."

Boffin looked at Tom.

"He doesn't drink orange juice, Mum."

"Oh, well, I'll fetch something else. What would you like?" She waited for Boffin to answer. He stared back.

"Maybe some water?"

Tom jumped up to follow her out to the kitchen.

"Mum," he said softly, "Finn's very tired. Do you mind if we eat in my bedroom? I think he'd be happier. He's a bit shy."

"Yes, I can see that. He's hardly spoken a word yet. Poor boy! Go on, you go up. I'll explain to Dad."

"Thanks, Mum!" Tom gave her a quick hug.

He helped Boffin up the stairs and closed the bedroom door after them.

There was a knock almost immediately. It was Dad with a tray. On it were two plates of steaming pasta, two bowls of mixed salad and two tall glasses of water.

"There's strawberries and cream for afters. I'll bring them up later."

"Thanks," said Tom, taking the heavy tray. "This looks great. Doesn't it, Finn?"

"Looks great," said Boffin. "Thank you."

Dad beamed. "Dig in while it's still hot and shout down if you want seconds."

Tom clicked the door closed with his foot and carried the tray over to his desk by the window.

"I guess you don't eat real food?"

"No. Ishi Kashikoi eats lots of burgers. Humans eat food for energy. But Boffin will need energy soon. Levels are getting low. Look!" He pulled up his jacket and showed Tom a discreet glass panel on the left side of his hard plastic chest. Tom pushed a mouthful of pasta into his mouth and bent forward to have a look. Boffin hooked his fingers under his rib cage and a rectangular piece of chest swung open.

Tom inhaled sharply and choked. "What are you doing?" he coughed.

"Showing Tom where battery charger is."

There, in a neat compartment in Boffin's chest, was a coiled up wire with a three-pinned plug on one end. Boffin closed the door again, and then pointed to his tummy button.

"This is where charger lead goes. Here."

"Fascinating! But pull your jacket down, before Dad or Mum walk in."

Tom looked up and found Boffin watching him intently, following each forkful to his mouth and imitating the chewing motions.

"Do you want to look at a comic or something?"

"Yes." Boffin nodded his head vigorously.

"Here, there's a pile on the bed."

Tom watched Boffin sift through the comics, then choose one and sit down on the rug with it. He glanced at him from time to time while he ate – first his plateful of pasta, then Boffin's.

"I'm not going to be able to eat another thing. I'll go and tell them we're full. Mind out of the way, Boffin. I'm coming through with the tray."

Boffin slid over, but didn't look up from his comic.

Tom found him in the exact same position when he got back a few minutes later. It was the first moment all day that Boffin had looked relaxed. Tom got out his felt pens and paper, spread them in an arc on the floor and lay down on his tummy. Then, without thinking, he began a new cartoon character for 'Robot Zone'.

It took him a moment to realise that Boffin had stopped reading and was watching him. "No, don't move!" said Tom. "I'm drawing you."

"Drawing! Can Boffin draw too?"

"Sure! Here's some paper. Use any pen you like."

Boffin lowered himself, tummy down, on to the floor. With the very smooth movements that Tom was starting to take for granted, the robot picked up a thin sheet of paper between thumb and forefinger and placed it neatly in front of him. He chose a black marker and pulled its lid off. *Squeak, scratch*, went the

marker. With a few deft movements Boffin finished his drawing. It was a perfect likeness of Tom.

"Here," said Boffin. "A present."

Tom took the sheet. "It's good. Really good."

"Boffin likes doing pictures."

"Do you want to work on the comic with me?"

"Yes," said Boffin and clapped his hands. "Oops, sorry, forgot. Boffin must not clap hands again. It's hard to unlearn something."

"It's okay. Didn't mind that time, just don't do it in front of anyone else. Looks weird!"

"Okay, Tom."

Tom hadn't enjoyed himself like this for ages. Not since before they moved here. They drew for most of the evening, until Mum made Tom jump by suddenly sticking her head around the door.

"Tom, can I have a word?" She beckoned him out on to the landing, waited for him to join her and then latched the door. "I'm surprised that Finn's parents haven't telephoned."

"They're probably still travelling. Don't worry, Mum. They know he's fine with us."

"Well, I am worrying. Poor boy, he must be too. What time are they coming for him tomorrow?"

"Oh no, they're not picking him up tomorrow. Didn't I tell you? I don't know how long he'll have to stay for.

It depends on how er . . . sick . . . his, er, aunt is. That's okay, isn't it, Mum?"

Mum's shoulders dropped. "Well, yes. Of course we'd like to help. But I would like to talk to them myself, just as soon as possible, to have some idea of what's going on."

Tom flushed so hot, it felt like he'd turned into a radiator.

"Don't look so worried," said Mum. "I'll ask Finn for their telephone number. I'll leave it for tonight, but it would be good to talk to them first thing in the morning." She opened the bedroom door and asked, "Would you like a drink, Finn?"

Boffin shook his head.

"Me neither," said Tom, "but thanks." He dropped down beside Boffin on the carpet and pretended to be happily drawing again. But really he was worrying about the telephone number and hoping that Mum would go away, so he could think. She did, but seconds later he heard Dad's heavier footfall on the stairs.

"Bedtime, you two!" Dad poked his head around the door.

"Aww!" said Tom.

"Aww!" said Boffin.

"It's school in the morning. I'm going that way tomorrow, so I could drop you both off. Save you a walk."

"No!" Tom said a little too abruptly. He couldn't take Boffin to school with him. It would be a total nightmare. "We'll walk. But thanks." Tom's mind filled with images of Jack guessing straightaway and revealing Boffin to the whole class, then the class pointing and laughing, and Mr Richardson being furious.

Dad's voice brought him back. "Okay. Whatever suits you."

He saw his dad do a double take. "What's happening here?"

"Nothing."

"Doesn't look like nothing to me."

"Oh, you mean the drawings. We're making up new characters for the comic."

Dad bent to scoop up a handful of papers. "These are brilliant! You really should pack up now . . . but you can have an extra few minutes, because tomorrow you might not be in the same groove at all and these are fantastic. It's really funny, the idea of a robot coming to life like that!"

Chapter Six

Tom couldn't get to sleep. It was the middle of the night and his parents had gone to bed ages ago. Boffin was motionless on the fold-up bed beside him, with a black flex sticking out of his tummy button and winding its way up over the pillow into a wall socket. Tom was watching and listening for any movement on the landing. There was no way he wanted his parents to walk in and find this scene. They would freak out.

He'd already had to get up and chuck a duvet over the robot when he heard Mum or Dad go to the bathroom. By the time they'd returned to their bedroom Boffin was overheating and making a terrible noise again. Tom had pulled the duvet off and waited anxiously with it in his hands, in case his parents came to investigate. They didn't and finally he got back into bed.

"Boffin! Wake up!"

It took a few seconds for the robot to respond.

"What does Tom want?"

"It's all right for you, you're able to just switch off and go into sleep mode – but I can't!"

"Why not?"

"I'm afraid Mum or Dad are going to come in and see you, looking like that. You look so weird. Hasn't your battery charged enough yet?"

"No. It will take all night."

"Not a very good design," said Tom.

"Yes it is," said Boffin.

Tom thumped his pillow to make it more comfortable, but the harder he tried to sleep, the more wide awake and crosser he became. "This isn't working. It just isn't. You're going to have to go back to the museum tomorrow."

"No!" cried Boffin, sitting up so suddenly that he pulled the plug from the wall.

"Sshh! They'll hear you. Now look what you've done." Tom swung out of bed. "Lie back!" He put the plug back into the socket.

"Don't want to go back to the museum, ever. Doesn't Tom like Boffin any more?"

"It's not that. It's really cool having a robot to stay. But I hate having to lie to Mum and Dad. And they're too smart, they'll find out. And what about tomorrow? You can't come to school with me."

"School! Boffin would love to go to school."

"Well you can't. No way and that's final."

"Want to," said Boffin.

"Oh, go back to sleep!" Tom pulled his own duvet over his head and, after thinking hard about what to do in the morning, reached for his alarm clock and set it for six o'clock.

*   *   *

"Tring! Tring! Tring!" Tom woke with a start. Feeling around for the clock under his pillow, he found it and switched the sound off. *Eurgh*, it was much too early to be awake.

But Tom knew he had to get Boffin out of the house before Mum or Dad were awake. He let out a low groan of tiredness. Tom thought through his plan: to take Boffin to the shopping mall and lose him there. But his brilliant idea didn't seem so good this morning.

What else can I do? I can't leave him at home. An image of Mum's ruined flowerbed came to mind. He'd wreck the place. It's going to have to be the shopping mall. Then I can phone the museum, without giving my name, and let them know he's there. They'll come and collect him.

Tom swung out of bed. The first things he noticed were the pages of comic on his bedside cupboard, the ones from last night.

Boffin whirred into life. "Good morning!"

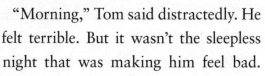

"Morning," Tom said distractedly. He felt terrible. But it wasn't the sleepless night that was making him feel bad. It was the whole mess he'd got himself into. "Can I unplug you now?"

"Yes, thank you," Boffin said, rubbing his tummy and smacking his lips, as if he'd just had a tasty meal.

Tom laughed.

"Why is Tom laughing?"

"I think you're great. You look so human."

"Tom getting mushy again."

"Yeah, a bit." He leant over Boffin and unplugged him from the wall. "Here."

Tom handed the three-pinned plug to Boffin, who sat up and pulled the other end of the flex out of his tummy button. He rolled it up, opened his chest and stuffed it in.

"*Euch!*" thought Tom. He hated to see the chest cavity open like that.

Boffin levered himself off the bed and stood up.

"You need clothes," Tom said. He opened the black bin bag that he'd discovered yesterday. "I remember these," he said, pulling a pair of jeans out. "They'll do. Try them on, see if they fit."

Boffin took the jeans and slipped them on.

"Do the zip up."

"Zip! What is zip?"

"That." Tom pointed. "Oh here, I'll show you. Just this once, okay? Watch carefully, because I'll never do this again." Tom pulled up the zip and fastened the button on the waistband. "They fit. Good! Just one more thing!" He got a pair of scissors and cut a small rectangular hole over where the air vent was.

"Boffin likes wearing clothes, feels like real boy now." He stroked the jeans.

"You'd look better with a shirt on. This one will do. No, don't tuck it in. We need to cover the hole I just cut. You're ready." Tom smiled. "My turn now – I need to go for a shower, okay? Do you want to do some more pictures while I'm away?"

Boffin nodded, sat cross-legged on the floor and picked up the pen he'd been using last night.

Tom went through to the bathroom and turned the shower on. As soon as it was hot enough, he got under the spray, squeezed a dollop of shampoo over his head and worked up a lather. Just as he was about to rinse he heard a loud crash. Tom quickly turned the tap off and stood shivering, listening intently. Seconds later came a loud *thump*, *thump* on the door.

"Tom! Tom!" It was Boffin.

He got out of the shower and the soap suds from his head plopped, in meringue shapes, on to the bathroom floor. He skidded on one and stubbed his big toe on the side of the bathtub. "Aagh!"

"Tom! Tom!"

"Just a minute. Sshh! Keep your voice down," Tom hissed through the door. "I'm coming." He stuck his soapy head out. "What's wrong?"

Then he saw Dad appear on the landing, rubbing his eyes and squinting at them.

"What's up? What's all the din?"

"Nothing, Dad, it's okay." Tom grabbed a towel, threw it over Boffin's bald head, totally encasing it, and pulled him into the bathroom. "He got soap in his eyes."

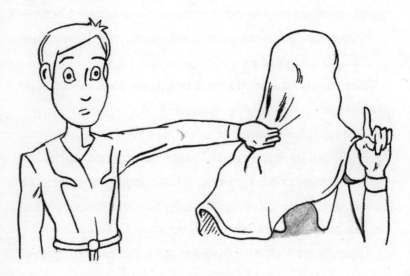

"Is that all? I thought I heard a loud crash."

"Just us. Sorry for waking you."

"You do know that it's just after six, don't you?"

"Yeah. Thought we'd get up early. I want to show Finn around before we go to school."

"Not much to see locally, is there? But it's up to you. Just keep the noise down a bit. Mum's still asleep."

"Yeah, sure. Sorry about that."

Boffin was struggling to get free, but Tom held on tightly to the towel.

"Can't see!"

Tom squeezed the towel tighter around Boffin's head, trying to muffle his voice further.

"Sshh!" he said under his breath, locking the bath-room door with his other hand. He gave Dad a couple of minutes to get back to his bedroom, then released Boffin.

"Tom has no clothes on. Looks funny."

"Shut up! Just shut up!"

Boffin curled himself up into a tight ball.

"What are you doing that for?"

"Tom said *shut up*."

Tom took a deep breath. "Stop that and get up! What was the loud crashing noise? What have you gone and done now?"

"Didn't mean to. It was an accident."

Tom didn't wait for any more information. He opened

the door again, checked that there was no sign of Dad, grabbed Boffin's arm and pulled him along the landing to his bedroom.

He saw immediately what had happened. The shelf over his bed with all his robots on had come down from the wall and the models were strewn everywhere. His favourite one, the Moonwalker, was halfway across the floor with its arm missing. He bent to pick it up.

"How could you? I asked you not to touch them. You're a bad robot!"

Boffin bowed his head.

"How did you knock the shelf down?"

"Wanted to do drawing for Tom, of his special robot, but Boffin's foot slid on a comic and I went flying like bird into shelf and . . ."

"Okay. Stop. I s'pose you didn't mean it."

Tom picked up the models and all the broken bits and put them on his desk. He propped the shelf up against the wardrobe.

"Will Tom be able to fix robots? Boffin could help."

"No, you've done enough. Look, I'm freezing. I've got to go and rinse this shampoo out of my hair. So I'm going to have to leave you on your own again. This time I want you to sit down on the bed. Good! Don't move! Not one muscle! I mean it, Boffin. You're not to move from that spot till I get back!"

"Yesh," said the robot through tightly clenched teeth.

"And put your hat on! Dad nearly saw you without any hair."

"Can Boffin move to get hat?"

"Yes. It's on the end of your bed. Here!" Tom handed it to him and Boffin pulled it on.

"But from now on, do not open your mouth and do not move!"

Back in the bathroom, Tom was as quick as he could be, but as he was drying himself he heard someone walk past the door. He stuck his ear to the door and heard Dad's low rumbling voice. He was talking to Boffin.

"You don't have to wait up here for Tom. You're welcome to come down and start breakfast."

No, Tom thought.

"Ton said not to oove."

"What was that?"

"Ton said not to oove." Boffin said louder. "Ton said not to oove!"

"Oh, Tom told you not to move?"

Tom tied the towel round his waist and rushed out.

"Yesh!" Boffin was nodding his head. "Oh oh! Ooved."

Dad laughed and walked towards the door. "Your

friend's been entertaining me." Then he whispered as he passed, "I don't understand a word he's been saying. See you both downstairs in a few minutes."

Chapter Seven

"I thought we'd never get away." Tom hoisted his bag up higher on his back as they walked along the pavement. "When Dad offered, did you have to say yes to more toast? I hope he didn't see me putting it into the bin. I couldn't eat it." His stomach was churning, like it had been all morning. It was the same kind of feeling that he got before exams.

"Won't do it again," said Boffin. "What's it like to eat?" He made chewing motions, up and down with his jaw.

"Stop that! It looks weird."

"Okay." Boffin fell into step beside him. Tom couldn't think of anything else to say.

"Your Mum and Dad are nice people. Tom is lucky. Boffin is happy being in a family. Tom is like Boffin's father."

It was as if the robot was sensing the dark deed that Tom planned for him. Tom kept his eyes on the pavement ahead and they followed it around into the mall.

His plan was to take the robot down to the furthest end of the covered arcade and into a bookshop. There he would lose him in amongst the tall bookcases. It would be easy. He'd be out of there and away before Boffin would notice. All he had to do then was phone the museum from a public phone. And there was one just out of sight around the corner.

"Uh-oh! That's all we need," said Tom. What was Jack doing at the mall before school? "Stay quiet, Boffin, don't say a word to this guy! Okay?"

"Well, look who's here. It's lickle Tommy Wommy with his new friend. They're very good friends, I heard." Jack elbowed Harry, the big brown-haired boy with him. "Know what I mean?"

Harry laughed, revealing big teeth which seemed to take up most of the lower part of his face.

"I saw them holding hands yesterday," continued Jack, falling into step beside Boffin. "New, aren't you? You can't be all that bright if you pick Tom as your friend."

Boffin stayed quiet.

"Push off, Jack!" said Tom.

"Oh, so Tommy's feeling brave. That's new."

"It's not new Jack. In case you're too dumb to have noticed – you're not important enough for me to bother with."

"Ooohh. I'm hurt. You're breaking my heart!" said Jack, walking backwards and holding on to his chest.

Boffin turned around and mimicked him. "Ooohh. I'm hurt. You're breaking my heart!"

Jack's face pulled tight in fury. He caught hold of Boffin's jacket collar. "Right, mate! Think you're clever, do you?"

"Yes, Bof—"

Tom dropped his bag. "Leave him alone!"

"Shove off!" Jack shouldered Tom, knocking him off balance. "This is between me and your friend."

"Oh, stop being such a jerk!" said Boffin.

"Take this, big mouth!" Jack punched him hard on the chest. "Ahh!" he cried, drawing his fist back. "Ahh!" he cried again, hugging his hand to him.

Harry tucked his teeth behind a thin grimace, but stood there, clearly unsure what to do.

Boffin walked up to him. "What funny teeth you've got. You look like a donkey!"

Tom saw Harry's fist clench.

"That's enough, Finn." Tom caught hold of Boffin's arm and pulled him away.

"We'll get you later!" Harry shouted after them as they left the shopping mall.

"Those boys are silly," said Boffin. "That big boy has funny teeth." He imitated Harry's grimace perfectly.

"Stop it! Please stop!" spluttered Tom. "They'll kill us if they see us laughing." He tried not to look, but

Boffin wouldn't stop. The more Tom laughed, the more the robot pulled his top lip back.

His plan to get rid of Boffin hadn't worked. Jack turning up like that had blown the whole thing – but it had also shown Tom that maybe, just maybe, he'd get away with having Boffin alongside him at school. Jack hadn't a clue who Boffin was and, if he didn't recognise him, then the others might not either. Tom felt a surge of bravery. Boffin had been brilliant back there with Jack. If he just did what Tom said, they could get away with it. He was going to take Boffin into school with him.

Blending in and moving with the crush of pupils around them, Tom guided the robot through the large glass doors. He tried to shield Boffin from being jostled out of the way. The robot's eyes were darting everywhere.

"So many," he said. "Big ones, little ones. Hairy ones, right down the back." Boffin pointed to a girl with long brown hair. "Why do some girls have hair right down there? Is it to keep them warm? And why is that boy's hair sticking up? And why doesn't Boffin have hair?"

"Cool it! Stop with all the questions and keep your voice down!"

"Boffin wants hair. Long hair – like that girl. See!"

"Don't point! Try and act normal."

"Boffin likes that girl." He started walking towards her.

"No!" said Tom, catching hold of Boffin's arm. "You've got to calm down, or I'll take you back to the museum, right now."

"Boffin is trying to learn new things."

"I know, but you've got to be clever about it. Look and listen, but stop acting like an idiot. See! No one else is fussing about hair and chasing girls. They're all in a hurry to get to class. You've got to be quiet and blend in, or they'll know that you're not one of them. You can't behave like a robot here."

Boffin nodded slowly. "To be like other boys, Boffin needs hair!"

"You're okay as you are. Stop worrying."

Boffin went to lift up his hat.

"No, don't take your hat off. You mustn't, no matter what."

"See, Boffin not okay without hair."

"Will you stop going on about hair. It's boring."

"Boring?"

"Shut up!"

The robot started to curl himself into a ball.

"No, don't start that again. Everyone's starting to look at us. Please, if you're really good I'll find you some hair."

Boffin immediately unfurled.

"Tom is good dad."

"I'm not your dad. I'm just your friend! Come on, the bell's about to go."

"Bell. Why is bell important and where is it going?" asked Boffin.

"Huh? What are you talking about now?"

"Tom said the bell's about to go. Where?"

"Nowhere . . ."

"But you said . . ."

"I meant it is about to ring, to make a sound, okay?"

They joined a line of pupils trying to get in through the classroom door. Jack and Harry had somehow got there ahead of them.

"Hello, Jerk," said Boffin.

Jack narrowed his eyes at him, but to Tom's surprise stepped back to let them through. As Tom passed, Jack whispered in his ear. "Think you can hide behind your friend, do you? Watch your back. When you least expect it, I'll get even."

Chapter Eight

"Settle down, everyone! Quiet!" Mr Richardson placed a pile of books on his desk. "I want you to do a short piece of writing, no longer than five hundred words. I want you to write about our visit to the museum yesterday. Think about it as a diary entry and try to record our trip in as much detail as you can."

"Ah, Sir!" groaned Jack from the back of the classroom.

"Ah, Sir, what?" Mr Richardson looked across the heads in his direction. His eyes stalled on Boffin.

"A new student! How come I wasn't told to expect you?"

Boffin sat motionless.

"What's your name?"

Boffin blinked.

"Well?"

"His name's Finn, Sir," said Tom, his voice coming out louder than he'd expected.

"Thank you, Tom. But can't he speak for himself?"

"He doesn't speak much English. He's from Japan."

"Doesn't look Japanese to me," said Jack.

"That's enough!" barked Mr Richardson. Tom saw a fleeting look of annoyance pass over his teacher's face, quickly replaced with his I'm-ever-so-patient smile. "Well, class, get on with your writing, while I go and have a word with the headmistress. Tom, will you make sure . . . what did you say his name was?"

"Finn, Sir."

"Make sure Finn has everything he needs."

"Yes, Sir."

"Yes, Sir!" Jack repeated.

"Sshh, that's enough! Get your books out and start work."

There was a scraping of chairs and a clunking of bags on desktops while notebooks were taken out. Tom saw his teacher wait for silence to descend, then quietly slip out of the classroom. *Thump, thump, thump,* Tom's heartbeat started to race. *Thump, thump, thump, thump.* The headmistress's office was just down the corridor.

A girl who sat at the desk in front of them swung around. Her long brown hair swished out, before settling like a cloak on her back. "Hello, Finn. My name's Sasha." She smiled. Boffin smiled back.

"Careful," called Jack. "Tom'll get jealous." Harry, sitting near Jack, tittered.

A look of embarrassment spread over Sasha's face, and she turned her back on them.

Tom was watching the door, waiting. There was a tap, tap on his shoulder. He glanced sideways at Boffin.

"Yes?"

"Need book and pen."

"Sorry. Yes." He bent down to get a spare from his bag. "Here," he whispered, sliding a red pad and pen on to Boffin's desk. "Draw a picture of a robot, like the ones we were doing last night."

Boffin lifted his hands as if to clap.

"Don't! No clapping here, okay?"

Boffin pulled his bottom lip in and nodded.

Tom felt much too tense to write. He knew that any second now, he could be in for it. What would the head-mistress and Mr Richardson do? How had he been so stupid? Why did he bring Boffin to school?

Tom stiffened as the door swung open, but it wasn't their teacher. It was Miss Murray, the classroom assistant. Tom liked her, she was friendly. "I'm standing in for Mr Richardson for a few minutes. If you need any help, just ask."

It was a bad sign, Tom thought. He tried to concentrate on his blank page. Boffin scribbled away, totally engrossed in what he was doing. It was the quietest

Tom had ever known him. He tried to see his paper, but the robot had his arm in the way.

"You all right there, Tom?" asked Miss Murray. "We're nearly out of time."

When he looked up she was facing the other way, wiping the whiteboard clean.

"I'd like to know how she does that," said Tom under his breath. "Must have eyes in the back of her head."

"Eyes in the back of her head! I didn't know humans had eyes in back of head."

"No! They don't."

"Tom said—"

"Shut up! And if you curl up now, I'll kick you."

"Oh, Tom," cried Boffin.

"What's going on over there?" It was Mr Richardson.

"Nothing!" Tom said quickly.

His teacher frowned at him. "Can I have less talking and more working? That goes for you too, Jack."

Tom sank lower into his seat. Silence settled around him.

"Thank you for covering for me," he heard Mr Richardson say quietly to Miss Murray.

"No problem. I hope you were able to . . ."

Tom strained to hear, but the noise of the class was building up again. He saw Miss Murray leave. Mr Richardson didn't seem happy. There was no doubt about it.

His lips had tightened and he was tapping his desk with a pencil. He dropped it suddenly, got up and walked down amongst the desks, glancing at each student's work as he passed.

"Well done, Phil. Just have a think again about how you should spell acrobatic."

He paused when he got to Boffin. "I don't believe it!" Tom jumped.

"It's a perfect copy of the robot we saw at the museum yesterday."

"I can explain . . ." Tom stood up.

"No need. We can see for ourselves. Look, class, it's the free-thinking robot!" Mr Richardson held Boffin's notebook up.

Tom sat down quickly. Boffin had done a line drawing, showing every work-ing part, clearly labelled and

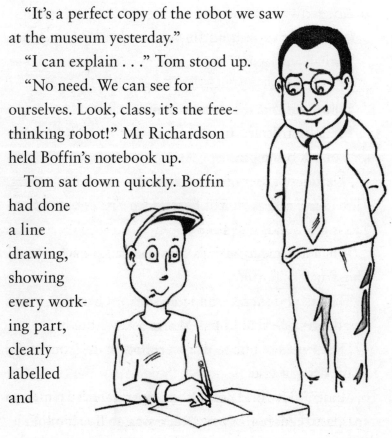

numbered. There were exact measurements of the robot's height, width and weight. He'd written a date given for its life expectancy and even an address where spare parts could be bought from.

"How come you know so much, or is this just a terrific imagination?" Mr Richardson looked eagerly at Boffin.

Here it comes. Tom wished he could melt away. Just disappear without a trace.

"You must've seen Boffin Brainchild at the museum, or perhaps in Japan?"

Don't speak! Don't speak! Tom willed him.

Boffin didn't. He sat there motionless.

Mr Richardson's tiny smile said it all. The teacher was out of his depth.

"He doesn't seem to understand a word I'm saying. Here, have a look at it!" He handed the book to Tom. "Pass it around, will you?"

When it came to Sasha's turn she gazed back, totally awestruck at Boffin.

That's all I need, thought Tom. When class was finally over, he had to pull Boffin away from her.

"But I wanted him to draw a robot on the front of my book," Sasha said.

"Later!" Tom held Boffin's arm tightly and led him from the classroom. Boffin wriggled, trying to free himself.

"No!" said Tom. "You're coming with me."

"No, want to do picture for girl."

"You can't!"

"Can."

"No, you can't!" Tom whispered fiercely. "Do you want to go back to the museum?"

Boffin stopped struggling. "No."

"Well, be good then!"

"Just a minute! Finn, Tom!" Mr Richardson came hurrying after them.

"Oh no," said Tom.

"Oh no," said Boffin.

"I need a word."

"Any word?" Boffin asked.

"What?"

"Sshh!" Tom narrowed his eyes in warning. The robot copied him.

"This is all highly irregular," Mr Richardson said, concentrating on Tom. "I haven't been able to have a word with the headmistress, because she's at home with a bad migraine. No one else was told to expect a new student today, either. The school secretary has checked her records, and there's nothing there on Finn. It's a real mystery. Is there anything else you can tell me about him? You seem to be the only one with any information."

"I don't think I *can* tell you much more about him."
Tom swallowed hard.

"In that case, as it's Friday, we'll have to wait until
Monday morning. Tom, will you do me a favour?"

"Yes, Sir."

"You are somehow managing to communicate a bit
with him. Can you show him around and make sure he
knows which room he's meant to be in?"

"Yes, Sir."

"And one last thing. As you know, we have a 'No
Hoodies, No Hats in School' rule." He smiled as if to
soften the message. "Get Finn to remove his hat please."

"No, Sir. He can't." Tom thought quickly.

"Why not?"

"He . . . he seems embarrassed about it. I tried to get
him to take it off already, but . . . he . . . hasn't got any
hair."

"Oh! How unusual. But it does happen, I know." Mr
Richardson bent down to Tom and whispered, "Is he
unwell?"

"Don't think so. Maybe he was born like that.
Anyway, he seems scared of the others seeing him without his hat. He's afraid they'll make fun of him."

"Well, I suppose we could bend the rule for now, at
least until he's settled in. You know, Tom, he'll probably get teased regardless."

"Yeah, but this gives him a head start on it!"

Mr Richardson patted Tom on his shoulder. "Good one, Tom, 'head start', I like that. Got to take life with a sense of humour, that's my motto! Where would we be without it, eh? You'd better get back to your friend. He's looking a bit lost. Enjoy your break, Finn," he called, before walking away, his face back to its usual serious expression.

"Enjoy break? What is Boffin to break? This?" He reached out for a pottery ornament that Year 4 had on display in the main hall.

"No!" cried Tom, as it shattered on the polished cement floor. The students milling about at the other end of the corridor turned their heads to see what the noise had been.

"That was stupid of you!" Tom hissed. "You're such an idiot."

"Tom is always getting angry with Boffin. Shut up, he says. Come here! Do this, don't do that! Boffin is first free-thinking robot. Does not have to take orders from Tom! Can do things on his own."

"Well, if you're so clever, go on then. Do things on your own!" Tom walked away and went to the only place where he could get privacy – the toilets. He chose the fifth cubicle along and closed the door after him. He let the toilet lid down, sat on it and stared at the graffiti on the back of the door. He didn't read any of it, his mind was too full. *I'm sick of him. He's nothing but trouble. It would serve him right if he was found out.*

Thump, thump. "Where's Tom!" *Thump, thump.* The banging came closer and closer. "Tom! Where are you?"

Tom jumped up. "Oh, this is stupid! I can't leave you for a minute." He stuck his head out of the doorway. "What? Can't I even go to the toilet in peace?"

Boffin caught hold of Tom's hand.

"Cool it!" said Tom, shaking his hand free.

"Cool what?" Boffin asked crossly, copying the tone of Tom's voice.

Mr Richardson must have heard all the thumping and shouting. He walked in. "Everything all right?"

"Yes, Sir."

He looked at his watch. "Shouldn't you both be at your next class? Who do you have?"

"Miss Patten – for art," said Tom.

"Well, you'd better hurry up then. Do you want me to come along and explain about Finn?"

"No need, Sir. I'll do it. Come on, Finn. Now!" He held the door open.

"Quick," hissed Tom, "before Mr Richardson decides to follow us!"

They went out of the main building, across to a smaller one by the playing fields, and were the first to arrive in the art room. Boffin was fascinated by the pictures hanging on the walls. Tom noticed a stack of lino pieces on the teacher's table. "Great. I think we'll be doing lino-cuts today."

"What are lino-cuts?" Boffin put his head to one side and studied Tom's face.

"See the brown rectangular shapes over there? You cut designs into them with sharp tools and then coat them in paint or ink and print off a picture. Don't worry, I'll show you."

Boffin straightened his head and blinked. The classroom door burst open, spilling in noise and movement. Sasha was in front. She made straight for Boffin.

"This table's taken," Tom told her.

"So's this one." Jack banged his bag down on the table next to theirs. Scraping back a chair, he sat and lounged back in it.

Oh, perfect! Tom thought.

Sasha chose the table directly in front of Boffin. She kept flipping her hair over her

88

shoulder. Each time it landed on Boffin's table, lying there for an instant before sliding off to hang down her back again.

"Nice hair," said Boffin, his eyes following every movement.

"Yuck," said Jack.

"You're being too mushy," Tom whispered. "Stop looking at her like that!"

Miss Patten floated into the room in a long wispy skirt. She lifted a handwoven bag off her shoulder and hung it on the back of a chair.

"Good morning! Are we all ready to design and make our own prints today?"

The class murmured.

"Good! Jack, will you hand these out please?"

In the few weeks that Tom had been at this school, he'd noticed how Miss Patten always tried to get Jack to do something useful. He thought she was trying to win him over, but it made no difference. Jack treated all the teachers the same, as if they were annoying insects buzzing about him that he'd like to swat. She was holding out the lino pieces. Jack let his chair fall forward and got up slowly. He sniffed loudly as he took the lino pieces from her and then threw them one by one on to each table. When it came to Tom's turn, he threw it so hard that the corner hit Tom in the chest.

"Careful, Jack, we don't want any of them damaged," Miss Patten called.

What about my chest? Tom thought.

"I mean it, Jack. Be gentler with them."

Jack went to the other extreme and placed the remaining pieces down as if they were so fragile they'd shatter just as soon as they touched the table top. Tom saw Miss Patten raise her neatly plucked eyebrows, but instead of saying anything she opened a large bottle of black ink and began filling shallow trays with it. As soon as her back was turned, Jack threw a piece of lino straight at Boffin. It would have hit him in the eye if the robot hadn't reacted immediately and caught it in mid-flight.

"Hey, good catch!" said Tom.

"Tom getting mushy now."

"No, I'm not."

"Quiet please! Jack, surely you've finished handing them out. Sit down!"

Jack sniffed extra loudly as he sat down and Miss Patten handed out the engraving pens. She handed him one, then gave two to Boffin.

"Hand it across please," she said to the robot. Tom snatched the extra pen, waiting for Miss Patten to say something about the new pupil, but she just glided away to the next row.

She didn't even notice him! Tom had always thought that his art teacher was dreamy, and that she seemed to waft about in some other world. Now he knew it.

Sniff, sniff, snort. Sniff, sniff, sniff.

The noise was making Tom feel sick. He leant backwards in his chair. "Stop being so disgusting!" he said.

"Make me!" Jack sniffed louder.

Tom let his chair fall forward and tried to ignore the sound. He looked at Boffin. The robot was being very quiet. He'd copied Tom and placed his lino square in the middle of the table and sat waiting, watching Sasha intently as he did so. His eyes followed each movement as she swished her hair back over her shoulder. Watched the long tresses land on his desk for a second and then return to her back.

"Now," said Miss Patten, "I want you all to draw a simple

picture on a piece of paper. It can be of anything. A flower! A bird! Or you can draw a pattern. But to start with, I suggest you keep it very simple. Once you are happy with your design you can copy it on to your lino. You know where the paper is."

There was a loud scraping back of chairs as they all got up together.

"I'll get some for you," Tom said. "And you can choose a pencil." He pointed to pots of them on a side table.

Boffin looked pleased when he saw the colourful display of pens and rulers.

"We won't need all those," Tom said, when Boffin got back with his hands full of pencils, rubbers, rulers and paper scissors.

Jack was already drawing a skull and cross bones. At Tom's words, Boffin let go of everything he had in his hands. With a clatter it all fell on to Jack's table. Rubbers bounced off in different directions and pencils rolled on to the floor.

"Dweeb!" said Jack.

"It's okay," Tom said. "I'll get them."

He disappeared under the table and fished around with his hands to collect everything. As he popped back up, he saw something that he wished he hadn't. Boffin was poised with paper scissors, waiting. Sasha flicked

her hair back again. Quick as a meteor flash, Boffin swooped forward and cut a chunk out of it. Tom watched in horror as the rest of the hair returned to the girl's back.

Jack spluttered with laughter, sending a spray of spit on to his drawing.

"What is it, Jack? What's happening over there?"

"Nothing, Miss!" He wiped his mouth dry on his sleeve.

"Well, quiet please!"

Boffin, with a look of pure delight on his face, held the hair up to Tom.

"Got hair now. Just need glue!"

Tom snatched the clump and stuffed it into his pocket.

"That was stupid. You idiot!"

"Take no notice of him, mate," Jack said, nodding his approval to Boffin. "That was totally wicked!"

"Wicked," copied Boffin. He leant forward and cut a lump out of Jack's hair.

Uh-oh, thought Tom.

Chapter Nine

For one awful moment, everything seemed to be in pause mode. Tom saw the tuft of fringe in Boffin's hand and the look of shock on Jack's face. He waited for Jack to explode and pulverise Boffin. It wouldn't matter that they were in the middle of class.

As if someone had pressed the play button again, Jack's hand flew to his fringe and felt the gap.

"Totally wicked!" Boffin said. "Cool."

Jack gave a weak smile.

Tom snatched the scissors from the robot's hand.

"Give the scissors back!" cried Boffin.

"No!" said Tom. "And keep your voice down!"

"I will shout if Tom doesn't give the scissors back."

"You do and that will be it. We won't be friends any more."

"Don't care," said Boffin. "Jerk is my friend now." He draped an arm across Jack's shoulders. "You're my friend, aren't you?"

Jack nodded.

"If that's who you want as a friend, you're welcome to each other."

"Will you stop nattering over there?" Miss Patten glared at Tom. "What's got into you today? You're not concentrating at all."

"Sorry, Miss."

"Sorry, Miss," copied Boffin.

Jack smirked.

"Sorry, Miss," said Boffin again, this time doing the same hideous smirk.

"Shut up!" hissed Tom through stiff lips. He tried getting on with his work and ignoring them. It wasn't easy. Boffin made a sudden movement to pick up Jack's drawing, and quickly drew an exact copy.

"Hey, that's good," said Jack. "How about this? Can you draw one of these?" Jack drew a cartoon of Miss Patten. He gave her two big ears and a set of rabbit's teeth. She did have slightly bucked teeth and ever so slightly sticking out ears.

"Don't listen to him," Tom whispered. "He's going to get you into trouble. Draw something else."

95

Boffin put up his hand to stop Tom talking and started to draw again.

"Awesome!" said Jack.

Boffin slid an identical copy of Jack's grotesque cartoon onto Tom's desk.

"Take it away. What are you trying to do, get me into trouble? It's rubbish!" Tom scrunched the paper up.

Boffin banged his hand on his table. "It wasn't rubbish!" he said.

"Sshh!" said Tom.

"Image was good," Boffin whispered. "Tom not being nice."

"And you're being stupid!"

"Tom always saying Boffin is stupid. World's first free-thinking robot knows more than Tom does."

"Oh, really?"

"Jerk thinks Boffin is clever. Maybe Jerk would be better friend."

"Suit yourself." Tom turned away and stared at his blank piece of paper. Never before had he been stuck in art class. Boffin moved his chair closer to Jack. Tom glanced sideways. They had their heads close together, talking and laughing.

He'll probably tell Jack who he is, the stupid idiot. See if I care. I've had enough of him! I hope he gets sent back to the museum. It'll serve him right.

Tom drew a picture of an alien. It was a cross between Boffin and Jack. But the funny cartoon didn't make him feel better.

"If you're happy with your designs," said Miss Patten, "I would like you to copy them out on to your piece of lino. Then you can use the engraving tool to gouge out the lines. Take care not to let the tool slip, or you'll ruin the whole thing."

Tom looked about, at the pictures on the wall, hoping an idea would come to him. His eyes settled on a large poster of a hare. He did a lightening quick sketch of it, straight on to his lino, and felt pleased with how it had come out. He was about to show it to Boffin, but Jack was teaching him how to use the engraving tool. Tom couldn't believe it. Since when did Jack take time out to do anything for anyone else?

He got on with his own engraving, but he didn't enjoy it. The rest of the class dragged by.

It was a relief when Miss Patten called, "Time to clear up please. Jack, gather up the lino pieces and put them over there!"

"You can help me," Jack said to Boffin.

No, Tom wanted to say, but they were out of their seats before he got the chance. No one seemed to notice anything odd about the robot as he went around the class and collected the lino. Tom watched him follow Jack to a side table. They stacked up the lino into a mini tower. Boffin smiled in delight as he put the last piece on. Jack bent forward and said something in Boffin's ear. Tom knew, from the look on Jack's face, that he was planning trouble. He was certain it would be Boffin who would land right in it.

I don't care, Tom tried to convince himself, but he did. That was why he was sitting at the very edge of his seat and watching Boffin's every movement. Now, the robot and Jack had turned their backs to the class and stood close together. Tom could see their elbows moving, but he couldn't work out what they were up to. He looked at the clock. Mr Brown would be here any minute for their next class. Boffin had better sit down again and fast. Mr Brown was very different to Miss Patten. He wasn't dreamy. He was also a maths teacher, which meant he could count. He was bound to notice the extra student.

At that moment, Mr Brown strode in, ducking his head under the doorframe. In a strong Scottish accent he said, "In your seats, everyone! Nice to see that you've actually cleared up for once. I do wish there was another classroom vacant for us, but us wee beggars can't be choosers."

"What's that you said, Sir?" sniggered Jack.

"I know what you're thinking, my lad, and it's noo use. I'm up to your wee tricks. And if I have any more of them today, it will be out to the head teacher straight away with you."

"Head teacher," said Boffin. "A teacher of heads?"

Jack laughed.

"Another clever clogs come to join us. Just what I need! But I was told you couldn't speak English!"

Boffin looked at Tom and sucked in his lips.

"Sit down the pair o' you and no more antics," said Mr Brown.

Tom could see, as they walked back down the classroom, that Jack's trouser pocket was bulging and so was Boffin's. Mr Brown went to the whiteboard and started showing the class how to convert vulgar fractions into decimal ones. He was using a marker pen and it was squeaking away on the board. Tom's tongue had gone dry, as it always did. He hated that sound.

Suddenly, a small white object flew through the air, hitting the teacher on the back between his shoulder blades. Mr Brown spun around. "What was that?"

No one answered. Eventually, he went back to writing out the fraction.

"Your turn, Finn!" Tom heard Jack whisper.

Tom saw Boffin reach into his pocket and pull out a large rubber. They were the extra big ones Miss Patten usually kept on her desk. Boffin picked up a ruler and, as if he'd done it a million times before, flicked the rubber at Mr Brown's back. It hit him hard on the shoulder and then thudded to the ground at his feet. Mr Brown spun around and looked down at the object that had struck him.

"Right, that's enough. I want the person who threw this to own up."

Silence.

"If noo one owns up, then I will have to keep the whole class in until someone does so." He tapped his finger on the desk. "That means noo lunch."

"Ah, Sir," ricocheted around the room.

"I'm waiting."

Tom sucked in a breath and stood up. "It was me, Sir."

"Tom?" said Mr Brown.

"Tom did not do it." Boffin stood up alongside him.

"Sshh!" said Tom.

"Well, all I can say to you, Thomas, is that I'm very surprised and disappointed. You can go to the canteen and fetch yourself a sandwich, but you will have to come straight back here with it and stay in for the lunch break. Do you understand?"

"Yes, Sir."

"Sit down then!"

"Yes, Sir!" mimicked Jack.

"Yes, Sir!" mimicked Boffin.

Tom ignored them and tried to concentrate on the new maths, but all the time he was seething with anger. He glared at Boffin, but the robot didn't notice. He seemed fascinated by what Mr Brown was teaching them.

When the bell rang, Jack was first to his feet. He said to Boffin, "Coming?"

Tom busied himself with packing his books away into his bag. He wasn't going to plead with Boffin to stay. The robot could do what he wanted.

"No. I'll stay with Tom."

"Suit yourself," said Jack. "See you later."

Tom was pleased, but he wasn't going to show it. He concentrated on doing up the buckle on his bag.

Sasha walked past with her friend, Yasmin. Until then Tom had forgotten all about her hair. But there it was, swinging on her back. The gaping hole all too obvious to him, but it looked like so far Yasmin hadn't noticed it. She did though, as they reached the doorway.

"Your hair!" Yasmin squealed, pointing. "What's happened to it? There's a big chunk missing."

"What? You're kidding!" Sasha tried to look over her shoulder. "I can't see anything wrong."

Yasmin caught hold of a wad and dangled it up above shoulder height. "Look! There's a huge bit missing!"

"Oh, there is!" Sasha cried, staring at the shortened piece.

Tom caught hold of Boffin and pulled him back down into his seat. "Don't say a word." He put a finger to his lips.

Boffin tightened his lips and stayed motionless.

"What's wrong?" asked Mr Brown, walking over to the girls.

"My hair!" wailed Sasha. "It's ruined!"

"Ruined? What do you mean ruined?"

"I don't know how it happened?" Sasha sobbed. "I don't understand."

"Maybe you got it caught in something," said Yasmin.

"Maybe on the bus this morning? Did you feel a tug or anything?"

"No!" Sasha cried even harder.

"There, there," said Mr Brown. "Let's go to the office and see what's to be done." He turned to Tom, who tried to keep an innocent look on his face. "I'll be back in a couple of minutes, Tom. Wait there!"

"Yes, Sir!"

"Don't cry," soothed Yasmin. "It doesn't look too bad!"

"It does! It's awful! What's Mum going to say?"

Tom waited for the sound of crying to fade away down the corridor. Then he turned to Boffin. "This has been one of the worst days of my life," he said. "You've been nothing but trouble, Boffin! You can't go cutting people's hair off when you feel like it. Don't you see how unhappy you made that girl? It will take years for her hair to grow back again."

"Sorry," said Boffin. "Really sorry. Didn't know that. I didn't think."

"That's just it. You don't think before you do something. And why did you copy Jack and throw rubbers at the teacher?"

"Boffin learns by copying others."

"You can't copy everything other people do. What if someone jumped off a cliff, would you jump off too?"

Boffin blinked.

"There would be no more Boffin Brainchild if you did. You'd be in bits. Lots and lots of bits!"

"No more Boffin!"

"No more Boffin. So think before you do something, okay? And if you're not sure, ask me."

"Okay." Boffin was quiet for a minute. Then he reached out and touched Tom's head. "Would like to have hair like Tom's. Can you get me some?"

"Get off!" Tom laughed. "I give up. Come on, I need a sandwich . . ."

"Tom."

He looked up. It was Mr Brown.

"Just going to get a sandwich, Sir, then I'll be straight back."

"Straight back?" said Boffin. He ran his finger down Tom's spine. Tom pushed his hand away.

Mr Brown stared at Boffin. "Where are you from?" he asked.

"Japan, he's from Japan." Tom moved between them to stop Mr Brown from looking so intently at the robot.

"It's all right, Tom, you don't need to cover up any more. I know exactly what's going on here."

Tom went cold, a trickle of fear crawling down between his shoulder blades. Only Mr Brown and his mum managed to see right into his soul.

Mr Brown gently moved Tom to one side, saying, "I know that it wasn't you who threw that rubber." He looked deep into Boffin's eyes. The robot stared back. Tom watched as neither his teacher nor Boffin blinked. Mr Brown's eyes began to water, until he finally had to give in and blink several times to clear them. "Well, I don't feel happy about punishing the wrong person. So perhaps, young lad, you could help me and own up. I think it was either you or Jack. Which of you was it, eh?"

"He doesn't speak good English, Sir. Only in a kind of babyish way," said Tom.

"Not baby. First free-think—"

Behind Mr Brown's back, Tom shook his head frantically and covered his lips with his finger. *Sshh*, he motioned silently.

Boffin copied the movements. "Sshh!" he said to Mr Brown. Then he sucked in his lips and bit on them.

Mr Brown looked from one boy to the other. "Go on, get out of here, the pair of you, and don't let me catch you misbehaving again."

"But, Sir, you told me to—"

"I've told you to skedaddle!"

"Yes, Sir. Thank you, Sir!" Tom picked up his bag, caught hold of Boffin's arm and hurried him out of the art room.

"Skedaddle?" said Boffin. "What is skedaddle?"

"It means that Mr Brown has let us off the hook."

"What hook? Boffin isn't on hook. Hook is a bent piece of wire . . ."

Tom stopped and smiled sweetly. "Will you do something really clever for me?"

"Oh yes."

"Close your mouth – and keep it shut for the rest of the afternoon."

"Bo—"

"Ah, no! You're not to open it, not at all! For any reason."

Chapter Ten

"I'm glad that's over," Tom said as they walked between the tall school gates.

The pupils clumped into groups and went their separate ways.

"It's okay, you can talk now," suggested Tom once they were on their own again, walking along the path. He soon wished he hadn't, because all the pent up words came streaming out. At least if Boffin had been a human, Tom thought, he would have had to pause for breath.

"Boffin likes school, very exciting place, much better than museum. It's where to learn lots of new things – history, maths, art, geography, science. Science is easy to understand."

"Glad you think so."

"Boffin has learnt so much today. More than all my days at the museum. Tom was right to stop Boffin talking. I learnt more when I wasn't trying to think of words to say."

"So did I."

They turned the corner and saw Sasha and Yasmin waiting by the bus stop. As they came closer, Tom could see Sasha was crying again. Boffin stopped.

"Don't be sad," he said.

"My hair! It's ruined." She turned her head to show him the uneven ends.

"I'm very sorry," said Boffin, reaching out towards the hair.

Tom pulled on the robot's sleeve. Boffin shook him off.

"It's not your fault." Sasha gave him a weak smile. "I feel so ugly without my hair."

"No. You still have lots of lovely hair. Lots!" To Tom's horror, Boffin lifted off his baseball cap to show her his head. "No hair, see! *I'm* the ugly one."

Sasha's eyes grew wide. Her tears dried up immediately and she wiped the last traces of them away with the back of her hand.

"You're not ugly," she said gently. "Thank you for showing me. I think you're very brave." Her sad face broke into a sweet smile.

I don't believe it. She fancies him.

"Come on, Finn! Time to go home!"

"Bye." Sasha gave him a tiny wave, even though he was less than a metre away.

"Bye," said Boffin, copying her hand movements.

"Enough!" groaned Tom as Boffin kept looking back over his shoulder and giving the same little wave. "Stop it! It's embarrassing."

"Boffin likes that girl. She would make a good friend."

"It's not going to happen – forget it!"

"Tom is first member of Boffin's family and girl could be in it too. Boffin would like to have family of his own."

"No way!"

"Aaah!" said Boffin.

"Aaaah!" mimicked Tom.

"Aaaaah!" said Boffin.

"She wouldn't be so keen on you if she knew it was you who'd ruined her hair!"

"I said I was sorry."

"Yeah, I'm sure you are. But don't ever do that again, okay?"

"Okay."

"Good! I won't have to hide the scissors when we get home then."

They crossed over the road. Boffin was quiet for the rest of the walk home, which suited Tom, because the closer they got, the more worried he became. How were he and Boffin going to get through the whole weekend in the same house as Mum and Dad? For this evening, at least, his parents were working overtime and wouldn't be home until late. He just hoped he'd come up with some plans by then.

They'd arrived at the small iron front gate, which squealed on its hinges as Tom swung it open. Cue for Mrs Tyson to look out of her sitting room window. Tom waved at her. Boffin did too. Tom hurried the robot in through the front door. Mrs Tyson was nosey, but important. She was the reason that Tom was allowed to come home before his parents. He had his very own bodyguard, or at least that was how he liked to think of her – rather than his babysitter!

Mum had left a note on the fridge.

There's a ready-to-heat cottage pie on the top shelf and a salad. We shouldn't be too late. Do go round

to Mrs Tyson if you're bothered about anything or
phone me at work.
Hope you and Finn have had a good day at school.
See you later.
Mum x

Tom took a bag of crisps out of a cupboard and, standing with his back to the sink, crunched his way through
them. It took him a moment to realise that Boffin was
watching his every movement: how he took each crisp
out of the bag, put it into his mouth and chomped on it.

"Can I have one?" said Boffin.

"But you can't eat, can you?"

"I can't swallow, but I have teeth. Look!" And he
opened his mouth to show off a perfect set of molars,
realistic gums and tongue.

Tom handed him a crisp. "Here you go!"

Boffin took it between thumb and forefinger, held it up to the light and studied it, then put it into his mouth. *Crunch, crunch, crunch.* Round and round his mouth went.

"Feels funny!" he said, spraying crisp crumbs everywhere. "Boffin can hear noise from inside mouth."

"Stop spitting at me!"

"Sorry," said Boffin and spat it all out into his hand.

"Yuck! That's disgusting! Put it into the bin. And wash your hand."

Boffin rinsed his hands off under the tap.

"Here." Tom handed him a towel. "Do you want to work on the comic again? I'm supposed to be doing my homework, but I can do it later."

"Yes, I would like that, but can I take shoes off first?"

"Yeah, go on." Tom opened the fridge to pull out a carton of orange juice. "Look at all the food Mum has left for the two of us. No way can I eat all of that by myself." He slammed the door shut. "You okay?"

Boffin nodded. He was sitting on the floor, trying to pull his shoes off.

"They'd come off easier if you untied the laces first. Okay, maybe not! Well done. Come on then."

Minutes later, they were sitting cross-legged on the bedroom floor. The only sounds in the room were the crisps crunching in Tom's mouth and the scratching of pens on paper.

An hour passed very quickly.

"S'pose I'd better get on with my homework. Mum and Dad like me to get it done on a Friday. Then we've got the weekend to go places and do stuff. It's swimming tomorrow. You can come to watch if you want," said Tom from the doorway.

"Boffin would like that."

"I'll go get my work. Back in a minute."

When he returned with his bag, Tom found Boffin with the broken Moonwalker robot in his hand. He sighed. "Be careful. What are you doing with that?"

"Trying to fix it for Tom."

"Leave it! I'll look at it later, after I've done my maths."

Boffin put it down again. He walked around the room, and then round it again, as Tom got his books out of the bag. "Why don't you do some more of the comic?" said Tom.

"Want to work on it with you."

"I have to do this for now. Do you want to look at a book?"

"No."

"I'll try and be quick." Tom looked down at the long list of vulgar fractions. He was supposed to turn them

113

into decimal ones. If only he had been able to listen to Mr Brown during class, he might have some idea, but it was like looking at ancient Egyptian hieroglyphics. He looked in his text book to see if that would help.

"Boffin bored. It's like standing all day in the museum." The robot sank down on to Tom's bed.

"Sshh," said Tom.

There was silence for a couple of minutes, then, "Can Boffin do maths with Tom?"

"I don't think so," Tom laughed.

"Why laugh? Does Tom think I'm too silly to help?"

"I didn't mean that. But I need to concentrate."

Boffin got up and started walking round and around again.

"Okay, enough!" Tom threw down his pen and sat back. "Do you want to watch TV?"

"Yes! Boffin likes watching television. It helps me to learn."

"I'll see what's on." Tom opened a cupboard door by the foot of his bed to reveal his television and switched it on.

"A cartoon – is there a cartoon?" asked Boffin, standing far too close behind him.

"Boffin, give me some room." Tom flicked through the channels. "Nah, nothing any good."

"Boffin wants a cartoon!"

"Keep your hair on! Sorry. Oh, don't look at me like that. I've got some old DVDs in the spare room." He jumped up to get them.

"I think you'll like this," he said, coming back into the room and inserting a disc.

Boffin settled down cross-legged on the floor and gazed at the screen. Tom went back to his maths.

"Look, stars! Boffin likes stars. Good music, listen, Tom!"

"Uh-hum!" said Tom and put a line through his rough workings out.

"Ooh, Tom, clocks! Lots of clocks! Tick tock, tick tock, tick tock!"

"Sshh, I can't concentrate."

"Come look, Tom! Look!"

"I can't! I've got to do these maths questions and they're really hard. Please stop nattering at me."

"Sorry, will be quiet now." Boffin put his finger to his mouth and sshhed himself.

He was still for a few minutes, but then suddenly hopped up. Even with his head down, Tom felt Boffin standing there, staring at him. He looked up. "What?"

"I want to see your nose."

"Huh?" Tom went cross-eyed as Boffin's finger zoomed in.

"What are you doing?" Tom brushed his hand away.

The robot picked up a ruler and pressed its cold flat edge against the bridge of his nose.

"Quit it!" Tom snatched the ruler from him and put it down on his desk.

"Tom's nose isn't any bigger yet. When will it start to grow?"

"My nose has finished growing," said Tom.

"But Tom told lies."

"What are you on about?"

Boffin pointed at the screen. There, on pause, was Pinocchio. Boffin snatched up the remote control and deftly used it to rewind to where he wanted.

"Look!" he said.

Tom did, remembering the story. It was when the fairy asked Pinocchio questions and the wooden puppet lied in answer to them. With each lie his nose grew longer, until it looked like a tree branch.

"Oh, I see," laughed Tom.

"It isn't funny," said Boffin. "I don't like it. It's scary."

"It's only a cartoon. That doesn't happen in real life," said Tom.

"Are you sure?"

"Yeah. Watch the rest of it – it turns out okay in the end."

Boffin edged closer and closer to the screen as the story progressed. Tom tried to do the impossible fractions, but he just couldn't get them to work out. He took a sip of his orange juice and thought hard.

Boffin swung round from the TV, and stood over Tom again. Suddenly the robot plunged his finger into the glass on Tom's desk and, reaching up to his own face, dabbed the liquid under each of his eyes.

"Now what are you doing?"

The orange juice rolled slowly down Boffin's cheeks.

"Crying."

Tom looked at the sorry face with its orange tears. "What's wrong?"

"Pinocchio became a real boy, but I never will."

Tom didn't know what to say. After a pause, he plucked a tissue from a box on his bedside cupboard and wiped Boffin's face.

"But you're the best robot there's ever been. Come on, cheer up! Here, how about you helping me?" He angled his maths book around for Boffin to see. I'll turn the TV off."

Boffin looked at Tom's crossed out workings. "Tom is not doing sum right. When changing a fraction to a decimal, you should divide the numerator, the number on top, by the denominator, the number on the bottom."

The robot grabbed the pencil and Tom watched in awe as Boffin worked out the fraction in seconds. "How do you know that?"

"Boffin clever robot."

"Yes. I see! You're a very clever robot. Thanks for helping. I understand it now."

"Glad Tom is happy." Boffin sat down on the edge of Tom's bed and picked up a comic to read.

After a while Tom said, "I've done them. Let's go down for some supper."

"Can Boffin stay up here?"

"If you want to." He looked at Boffin's bent head. "You okay?"

"Yes." The robot carried on reading.

Tom hurried downstairs. He microwaved his meal. As soon as it pinged he grabbed a fork from the drawer and took the plate out, shovelling the food into his mouth quickly. It was far too hot, but he was aware that Boffin was on his own upstairs and no sounds were coming from there. It was too quiet.

Way too quiet, Tom thought as he raced up the steps, three at a time. He found Boffin standing by the window, staring out.

"What are you looking at?"

"The sky. I'm waiting for it to go black and then Boffin can see the wishing star."

"Wishing star? What wishing star?"

"In Pinocchio, the puppet maker wished on a star, for a real boy. The wish came true."

"That was just a story," said Tom. "Wishes don't come true like that in real life."

"Boffin wished to leave museum. That came true."

"But you can't even see the stars properly from here. The street lights are too bright. All you'll see is a yellow glow. You need to go somewhere away from big towns, like the Lake District – that's where you can see stars, billions of them."

Boffin walked to the door. "Let's go to the Lake District."

"Not now! It's too far away. It takes a whole day to get there."

"Oh," said Boffin.

Tom picked up his Moonwalker robot. "Do you want to help me with this?"

"Okay."

"Come on then!" Tom cleared the desk, pulled up

a stool for Boffin and took a small tool kit out of his bedside cupboard.

"Use this one." Boffin passed over a small-headed screwdriver. "Tom hasn't connected wires properly. Connect this wire to here and move that one to there, then arm should move."

Tom looked at where Boffin was pointing. He followed Boffin's suggestions.

He was almost finished when he heard a buzzing from his bag. Tom pulled out his phone. It was Mum.

"Just a minute, Mum," Tom answered. "I'm in the middle of something tricky." He tucked the phone between his ear and his shoulder.

"I'm in a hurry, Tom."

"I'll only be a minute, honest." He put the last wire into position, jumped up to get a battery from his desk drawer, slid it into a small compartment and switched the small toy on. It whirred straight into life.

"You're a genius! You're brilliant!" said Tom.

"Why, thank you, dear," said his mum.

"Not you. Finn! He's helped me fix my Moonwalker robot. It's working!"

"That's great, but listen. That phone number you gave me this morning, it doesn't work. I keep getting 'number not recognised'. Will you give it to me again and see if I wrote it down wrong?"

Tom couldn't remember the made-up numbers he had given her. "Call them out to me and I'll check."

Mum did.

"Try this," said Tom and altered two of the digits.

"Ah, I did write it down wrong. I'll try phoning Finn's parents now. You both doing all right there? By the sounds of it you are."

"Yeah, having a great time."

"Good. See you later. I won't be too late. Byee!"

Five minutes later, as Tom expected, she rang back. "That number still doesn't work, Tom!"

"Well, I don't have any other." Tom screwed his eyes closed and held his breath.

"I'll try the school instead and see if there's anyone still there. I might just catch one of the teachers. That's if I hurry. I'm not happy going into the weekend without speaking to Finn's parents. There's something wrong here. I just know it."

Chapter Eleven

Tom and Boffin were kneeling in the middle of the bedroom floor when Dad walked in. All about them were moving robots. Some were doing acrobatic flips. Others climbed up a ramp towards Tom's bed, crossed it, and then came back down a ramp on the other side.

"I don't believe it!" said Dad. "How on earth did you manage all of this?" He knelt down with them.

"It was him." Tom pointed at Boffin. "He's absolutely brilliant at building robots. Do you want to have a go? We're playing Robot Wars with these two."

"Love to."

A moment later, Mum appeared at the bedroom door. "Tom, I spoke to Mr Richardson and . . ." She stopped in her tracks. "You big baby," she said to Dad.

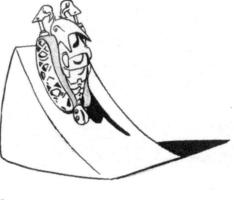

"You know you're just dying to get your hands on one of these. Come on." He held out a remote control. "I challenge you to a duel."

Mum looked uncertain for a moment, but then kicking off her shoes said, "Okay, you're on!" and knelt down beside him. "Hey, that's dirty!" she cried, as Dad's robot came crashing into the side of hers and sent it rolling over. "I wasn't ready!"

"Well, get a move on!"

"Which button do I press to get it to go forward?"

Boffin showed her.

"Thanks, Finn. Take that!" she said.

"Press that one. It makes the arm flip up." Boffin hovered near her.

Mum did, and it flicked Dad's robot over.

"Ahh, that's not fair! You had help."

Tom laughed and Boffin mimicked him.

"We're one-all. Next one wins," Dad said. His and Mum's robots chased each other around the bedroom.

Boffin jumped up and down in excitement.

"Now, Mum!" he called and she flicked the arm. Dad's robot went over again. Boffin clapped.

"Thank you," Mum beamed.

Dad put his remote control down. "Okay, I'm beaten. These are incredible! Where did you learn to make robots like this?"

"In Japan," Tom answered for Boffin, who had done his usual trick of sucking his lips in. Tom smiled at how ridiculous he looked and had to face the other way to stop from laughing. "He learnt all about robots when he was very young."

"Huh, some people get all the luck. That reminds me! You won't believe it, Tom, but that robot – you know, the one you went to see yesterday at the museum – has gone missing. I heard it on the car radio on the way home. It's been stolen."

Tom concentrated on the remote control in his hand. It began to shake. Boffin sat down beside him.

"Probably find out more about it tomorrow. It'll be in the papers."

Tom swallowed hard.

"Just imagine . . ." Mum looked at him intently. "You might have been one of the last people to see it." She transferred her gaze to Dad. "Do you think the police will want to question him?"

"I shouldn't think so. Exciting, isn't it?"

Tom tried to smile, but his face felt like plastic, all stiff and unnatural.

"I hate to be a killjoy." Dad tapped his watch. "But it's late. Time to put these little guys away."

"Ahh," said Tom.

"Ahh," said Boffin.

Mum whispered to Dad as they were leaving the room. "It's like having twins."

"Good fun, isn't it," Dad replied, clicking the door shut behind him.

Tom listened at the door to make sure they had gone downstairs. Then he turned to Boffin.

"We're in big trouble. There's going to be photographs of you in all the papers. Someone's going to recognise you. I just know it."

"But I don't look like Boffin Brainchild now. These

clothes make me look different. You said I look like a real boy now."

"I don't know," Tom said, unsure. "Your face is still the same. I'm scared – the police might come after us!"

"Boffin scared too. I don't want to go back to museum. Please don't send me away."

"I don't want to." Tom sat on the edge of the bed with his head in his hands.

"Don't be sad," Boffin said.

Tom felt a *thump*, *thump* on his head. The robot was trying to pat him better.

"Ouch, that hurts!" Tom ducked out of the way. "If you pat someone, you've got to be gentle."

"Sorry," said Boffin.

"It's okay," Tom smiled at him. "Come on, let's clear this lot away."

They lined up the robots on Tom's desk. Then he went and got a spare pair of pyjamas out of his drawer. He cut out a hole for the air vent and handed them over.

"Race you."

He let Boffin be the first into his pyjamas.

"Boffin won!"

"Go on, you can clap," Tom said.

"Nah, silly," said Boffin.

A knock came on the door. Mum stuck her head around it. "That was quick," she said. "Tom, will you help me with something?"

"Sure. Back in a minute," he said to Boffin. "You sit there."

"Yeah, what is it?" he asked as soon as they were out on the landing.

"I finally managed to talk to Mr Richardson."

"Oh?" Tom's heart started racing.

"He is totally in the dark too. He doesn't know a thing about Finn. And he had no idea that the boy was staying with us. He's waiting to talk to the headmistress on Monday morning and he hopes she will able to shed some light on what's going on here. Mr Richardson is just as worried as I am – Finn's parents seemed to have disappeared into thin air. I think I'd better come to school with you on Monday morning. We can't have the boy staying with us indefinitely, no matter how nice he is."

"No, I s'pose not." Tom wished that Boffin could stay. He wished that he could own up to his mother, right now, and beg her to let him keep the robot. But he knew she wouldn't let him.

"Oh, don't look so sad," Mum smiled reassuringly. "I didn't mean to worry you. I'm sure Finn's parents are fine – we'll probably hear from them tomorrow."

Boffin was in bed when Tom went back in. He felt so low that he couldn't look the robot in the eye, so he just switched the lamp off quickly and lay back on his bed. The bright street light shone in through a cherry tree and cast twiggy shadows on the ceiling.

"What are those?" asked Boffin.

"Shadows," said Tom. "Look, I can make shadows too." He put his hands together, flapped them, and there flying across the door was a bird.

"Oooh!" said Boffin. "How is Tom doing that?"

"Like this. You have a go." He showed him. Boffin copied the movements exactly, and a second bird joined the first one. The door opened and for a moment the birds fluttered across Mum's and Dad's faces.

"Goodnight," they both said.

Tom waited until he'd heard their own bedroom door close, then he got up and plugged Boffin in. "You're nearly flat!"

"Boffin not flat. See, Boffin has curves."

Tom laughed. "I meant you're nearly out of energy."

"Yes. I've been very busy today. It's been the best day ever." There was a gentle whirr and his eyes closed.

Tom lay back and yawned. It had been an amazing day. His brain flicked through images of all that they had done together. All the worries, all the lies he'd told, whirled about his head, until it felt like the room was spinning, but it wasn't. They slowed and calmed, like his breathing, and then he was asleep.

* * *

During the early hours of the morning, something woke him. He could see, through the gap in the curtains, that it was still dark outside. He turned over, and saw an empty bed. Boffin had gone.

"Boffin! Where are you?" He threw off the duvet and leapt out of bed.

The black flex which should have been connected to the robot's tummy was dangling over the edge of the bed and the door was ajar.

"Boffin?" Tom whispered, going out on to the landing.

The house was quiet. He felt a cool breeze eddying about his legs as he went down the stairs. The back door was wide open. His heart started racing. Boffin had left him, he'd walked out, just like he had done from the museum.

He rushed to the door. There was the robot, standing in the middle of Mum's flowerbed.

"What are you doing?" Tom tried to sound angry, but he was mainly just relieved that Boffin hadn't disappeared.

"Fixing the flowers, see!"

Boffin had a roll of tape in one hand and scissors

in the other. Tom took a closer look. Boffin had taped each shrivelled flower head back on to its stalk.

Tom grinned. "Ahh, well, Boffin, um . . . you can't fix flowers like that."

"But flowers are fixed. See!"

"You've stuck them back on, but they're dead. Look! All dried up." Tom brushed his fingers over one and the petals instantly fell to the ground.

"You've broken it again!" said Boffin crossly. He bent forward and began picking up each petal.

"No, leave them, Boffin. They're dead. You can't fix flowers like you can robots. They don't live for long after they've been picked."

"So I killed them? Bad Boffin!"

"No, you're not bad. You didn't know. And anyway, lots of people pick flowers all the time."

"Why?"

"To stick them in vases."

"Why?"

"I don't know, to make their houses look . . . pretty."

"I think that's silly!"

"It's just the flowers that have died, not the plant."

"Poor flowers." Boffin stroked each one.

"Okay, that's enough now. Back to bed!" Tom pointed to the door.

"In a minute. I want to see the stars first."

"But I told you, you can't from here."

They both looked up at the dingy yellow sky.

"See, there's nothing up there. It's cloudy tonight, but even if it wasn't, you wouldn't be able to see the stars properly. It's because of the street lights – it never gets dark enough. Sometimes, I can see the Plough, but we can't tonight, it's too cloudy."

"The Plough constellation is also known as Ursa Major. That's Latin for the Great Bear."

Tom's mouth dropped open. One minute Boffin was like a child, the next he sounded like a teacher.

"Okay, Professor Brainchild, it's time for you to go back to bed."

Boffin lowered his head and silently turned towards the house.

Tom followed. By the time he'd locked the back door and got upstairs, Boffin was in bed, his black lead plugged back into his socket.

"Goodnight," Tom said.

"Night."

And that was it. No more conversation.

Tom lay awake for ages after that. In the dark and quiet house he had time to think. He knew he couldn't keep Boffin for much longer. There was no way that Boffin could still be here on Monday morning. He certainly couldn't take him to school again.

131

Tom felt a pang. The same pang he'd felt when he'd seen the back door wide open and thought Boffin had run away. He thought of all that they had done for the last two days.

But he can't stay. Not with Mum on the case. And there's the newspapers tomorrow morning. What will they say?

Tom sighed. What a mess. How was he going to get out of it? It took him ages to come up with a plan that worked. He'd gone through several: one was to hide Boffin somewhere, ideally in a shed, and only allow him out after dark. But that would be cruel and too dangerous. Another was to be honest with his parents and ask them to help hide Boffin. But his parents would never agree to it.

Finally, he settled on this: on Sunday morning, he would put Boffin on a bus and then phone the museum to let them know where they could collect the robot from. No one would need to know where Boffin had been. Tom would have to make sure Boffin knew not to tell. He knew Boffin wouldn't like going back, but he thought he could make the robot understand. He'd promise him, and mean it, that he'd go and visit him at the museum.

In just two days, it would all be over.

Now that Tom had decided, he settled down under his

duvet. He wasn't happy – he wished there was another way. But there wasn't.

We've got tomorrow, and I'm going to make sure Boffin has the best day ever.

He turned over, faced the wall and finally fell asleep.

At around six in the morning, Tom awoke again to a rattling sound and a dull thud. The newspaper had arrived. He was out of bed and down the stairs before the paper girl had even got to next door.

There, on the front of the newspaper, was a photograph of Boffin Brainchild. His heart sank. As soon as his parents saw it they'd recognise the robot as Finn. Tom tore the page off. Flicking through the rest of the paper he found an article on page three and ripped that out too. He stuffed the rest of the newspaper under some magazines in the recycling bin in the garage. Then he padded up the stairs as quietly as he could. Boffin was still in sleep mode.

Tom turned on his bedside lamp and read what the torn out pages from the newspaper had to say. "Multimillion Pound Robot Missing" said the headline. *Uh-oh.*

He shook Boffin's shoulder.

"Wake up! We're in big trouble!"

Boffin opened his eyes.

"I didn't know you were so valuable. Look!" Tom held the article close to Boffin's eyes.

Boffin pulled his head back from it to focus properly.

"Keep it still, Tom. I can't read."

"You take it!"

Boffin started reading.

Tom, meanwhile, was out of bed and pacing the room. "You're going to have to go back right away. If they find out that you're with me, they'll think I stole you. And I didn't."

"No! I want to stay here."

Tom dragged his fingers through his hair, making the ends stand up.

"Please don't send me back. I'll be good. Do whatever Tom says. No cutting hair. No clapping."

"I don't want to send you back, honest. But you can't stay – not now. Not with you being in the newspapers. And my parents think you're only here for a couple of days. They're already worried about it. Then there's school. You won't be able to go there again."

"Why not?"

"Because . . . robots don't go to school."

"I did, yesterday."

"But only by me lying my head off. No, don't start looking at me like that. I know my head is still on."

"Boffin wants to stay with Tom and be part of his family. Never want to live in a museum again. I am happy here. I like being like real boy."

Tom looked away. Perhaps he could stick to his original plan. He only had to keep the secret for another day. One last day of having his own free-thinking, amazing robot – and of making Boffin happy. It was worth it, Tom decided. But come tomorrow morning, he would have to keep to his plan.

He got dressed, then helped Boffin with a change of clothes. Boffin was distracted by his new outfit and kept looking at his reflection in the mirror.

"Do you want to come to the swimming pool with me? It's quiet there, this early in the morning. Dad'll drive us. And I was thinking afterwards, we might go to the cinema. You'd like that. Lots to see."

"The cinema. Yes, Boffin would love to go to a cinema."

Tom smiled. "Come downstairs with me and help with breakfast. You can make Mum and Dad a mug of tea if you want."

"Really? Boffin has never made tea before."

"Well, you can this time."

Downstairs, Tom handed Boffin the electric kettle and asked him to fill it up from the tap. "You have to take the lid off. Yep, that's right. That's enough. Bring it over here."

Boffin sat it on its stand.

"I'll plug it in," Tom said. "Now, we empty the old teabags out of the teapot. See, into here." Tom put them in the bin. "And then we wait for the kettle to boil."

Boffin watched it carefully.

"I saw Ishi make tea in a big mug, many times, but he never let me do it. The water's boiling!" Boffin said as the kettle clicked off.

"Put the teabags into the pot then. No, that's too many. We only need two. Boffin, don't you miss Ishi?"

"No. Ishi Kashikoi is very clever man, but not a friend. He treats me, Boffin Brainchild, as big experiment. All the time testing me."

"You can pour the water in now. A bit more! That's enough. Put the lid on." Tom handed it over. "You

136

have to leave the pot for a couple of minutes. Then you can pour the tea into these mugs." He lined up two on the kitchen counter.

The robot stood by the teapot, waiting.

"Okay, you can pour now."

In his eagerness, Boffin tipped the pot up too far and the lid came off.

Hot tea poured all over the work surface.

"Oh no! Silly me!" Boffin put the teapot down. "Sorry, Tom!"

"It's okay." Tom grabbed a cloth from the draining board. "Ouch, that's hot."

"Boffin do it!"

"No, you finish pouring the tea."

"Tom still wants Boffin to?"

"Yeah. Just don't tip the pot up so high. Do it like this." Tom showed him, and then handed the pot over again.

Boffin poured very carefully.

"See, I knew you could do it. Here, put the milk in.

Just a little. Great! I'll take the mugs up, but I'll tell Mum and Dad that you made their tea."

When he came down a couple of minutes later, Boffin was pouring cornflakes into a bowl.

"They told me to say thanks and that it's the best tea they've ever tasted."

Boffin smiled. "Breakfast is ready."

Tom took the offered bowl.

"A spoon!" Boffin spun around and got one out of a drawer, handed it to Tom, then sat opposite and watched him eat. "Boffin could be good help about house, that's if Boffin stayed. Tom wouldn't have to do any work at all. Boffin could do everything."

Chapter Twelve

"Move over!" said Tom, trying to undress. They were in a changing cubicle at the swimming pool.

"Boffin can't. No room! Why is Tom taking his clothes off?"

"You know why. I've told you, I'm going for a swim."

"Fishes swim," said Boffin. "We had a goldfish in the lab. I liked to see it swim."

"Yeah, well, humans like to swim too."

"Why?"

"Because it's fun." Tom pulled his T-shirt off. "Right, I'm ready. I'll show you where you can sit."

He took Boffin to the door and pointed out. "See over there, above the pool, where all the seating is?"

"Boffin sees."

"You can sit and watch me, but don't talk to anyone. Okay?"

"Won't say a word."

"See you later."

Boffin nodded and walked away. Tom stood under

one of the showers and felt the warm water sluice over him. He was looking forward to his swim. After the warm shower, the cold footbath at the pool entrance was a shock. Tom rushed through it and turned to wave at Boffin. But the robot wasn't sitting where he'd told him to. He was standing by the rail with someone talking to him. It was Jack.

Boffin was shaking his head.

Tom had to get up there, and fast.

"Oi, no running!" shouted a lifeguard. "Look at the sign!"

What happened next seemed to go on forever. Tom heard a cry ring out as Boffin came flying backwards over the rail, over Tom's head, and with a loud splash

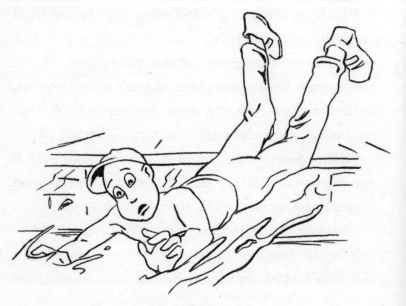

sank into the deep end of the pool. Tom, frozen in horror, saw the waters close over him. The lifeguard rushed past him and dived in.

"Hah, hah. Serves him right."

Tom looked up at Jack who was leaning over the rail. He felt like punching his grinning face, but it was too far away. Then he saw Jack's face freeze and his eyes grow wide.

Tom spun around. The lifeguard had surfaced with Boffin – but his body was lifeless. Another lifeguard appeared and helped to drag Boffin from the pool.

"Leave him alone!" Tom cried and tried to push them away.

"Don't be a fool, boy!"

Tom felt a strong arm grasp him across the shoulders and pull him backwards.

"Let me go! Let me go!" he struggled.

"No pulse!" said the lifeguard bending over Boffin, feeling his neck. "We're going to have to do CPR."

"Look what you've done!" Tom yelled up at Jack.

"Oh my God, I didn't mean to . . . it was only a bit of fun. He wouldn't talk to me." Jack backed away, falling over the seats behind as he went.

"Help me!" the lifeguard cried. "He's stone cold."

Tom was suddenly released. They tore open Boffin's shirt, the buttons flying everywhere.

"What's this, some sort of sick joke? It's just . . . a . . . dummy!"

"He's not a dummy!" shouted Tom. "Leave him alone!"

"Is he yours?"

"Yes," said Tom.

"I don't know what you were thinking of, mate, bringing a doll like this to the pool. I can see he's got electrics in him. You deserve a right telling off, wasting our time like this. Not to mention risking electrocuting everybody in the pool. And he's probably ruined now. Expensive kit that. Some kids don't know how to look after things."

Tom dropped to his knees. "Boffin!" he whispered into the robot's ear. "Say something!"

"I doubt if it'll work now. Not after being in the water. But we can't leave it here. Where do you want it?"

"I don't know," said Tom, shaking his head. He couldn't think straight.

"Let's take it down to the changing rooms. We don't want to leave it here, giving people a fright." The guard lifted Boffin up into a sitting position. "Give us a hand!" he said to his mate. "You take its legs. And you, young fella, get that hat out of the water!"

Tom knelt down and scooped up the baseball cap. He hurried after the lifeguards.

They sat Boffin in a cubicle.

"Right, he's all yours. Make sure you take him home with you. And never bring something like that here again!"

Tom waited for them to leave. As they did so, he heard one say, "That gave me one hell of a fright! Glad it was just a toy." Then he heard them laugh.

"Boffin, it's me. They're gone. You can talk now." But the robot's eyes stared straight through him. Tom could see that there was nothing there. No life in them at all. He didn't know what to do. He gently shook the robot. Boffin's head flopped on to his chest and he slumped to the floor.

"Get up! Get up, Boffin!"

The robot didn't.

"I'll dry you." Tom got his towel and wiped Boffin's face, hands and arms, but still the robot remained motionless.

Tom stood in the small cubicle with the robot at his feet. He felt as if the world was collapsing in on him. A terrible sense of panic welled up inside. It was as if someone had punched him hard in his stomach and he couldn't catch his breath. There was only one thing he could do now.

He phoned home.

Dad answered.

"What is it, Tom?"

"There's been an accident. Jack pushed Finn into the pool!"

"He's all right, isn't he?"

"No. No, he's not. Please come straightaway!"

Chapter Thirteen

"Say something!" Tom said.

Dad stood over him, filling up the entire cubicle door-way. He was staring at Boffin's crumpled form.

"I don't know what to say."

"Please, Dad. Help him!"

"Help him? How, for God's sake? He's a robot!"

"We need to get him home and dry him out."

"Have you any idea how I felt, as I drove down here? I went through a red traffic light and broke every speed limit. For this? And you stand there and tell me . . . that the boy we've had to stay in our house . . . that we've fed and looked after . . . is a robot! Just tell me, this isn't the robot that's been stolen from the museum."

Tom nodded his head slowly.

"Oh, Tom!" Dad dragged his fingers down over his cheeks, stretching his face into a grimace. "Do you have any idea what trouble you could be in? And what about Mum, and me? We've been harbouring stolen property and we didn't even know about it."

"I'm sorry."

"You lied to us!"

"I know," Tom said very quietly. The disappointment on Dad's face was too much, he had to look away. "It just kind of happened. I didn't mean it to."

"What? Do you take me for an idiot?"

"No! Course not. I didn't steal him, Dad. He came after me and before I . . ."

"Save your excuses, Tom."

"You've got to believe me."

"I don't think I'll ever be able to do that again."

"Okay! I'm sorry, sorry, sorry!" Tom's voice rose. "I messed up. I've ruined everything, but it's not Boffin's fault, it's mine – okay? And he needs our help. He can't talk any more or do anything. We've got to fix him. Please, Dad."

"Well, we can't just leave him here. Move out of the way and let me get at him."

Tom followed Dad closely as he carried Boffin up the steps and out of the building. Boffin's head hung limply over his father's shoulder and rocked from side to side. Tom had to run to keep up as Dad strode across the car park. They came to an abrupt halt by the car. Dad propped the robot up against it as he unlocked the back door. Then he heaved him on to the seat and with a loud bang slammed the door shut. Tom had never seen his dad look so angry.

"Get in!" Dad ordered.

Tom tried to tell his father about how Boffin had latched on to him at the museum and had then followed him on to the bus, but Dad stared mulishly ahead at the road. Tom saw a muscle twitch in his taut cheek.

"Not good enough, Tom," he said, changing gear. The car slowed down. "You should have told your teacher straightaway. He would have dealt with it and taken the robot back. But the thing that gets me most is why you couldn't be honest with us, your parents? I thought we had a better relationship than that. I thought we could trust each other."

Tom thought Dad couldn't say anything that would make him feel worse. He was wrong.

"As soon as we get home, I'm phoning the museum."

"Dad, no!"

"Yes, and that's final. The people at the museum need to know where their multi-million-pound robot is and I'd rather be the one to tell them, than to suddenly find the police on our doorstep. Have you stopped to think about the lifeguards? Don't you think they're likely to report today's incident? Don't you think they'll recognise it?" Dad used his thumb to point at the back seat. "Especially now there's a reward for any information!"

Tom stared out of the car window. It had begun to rain. "Do you think Boffin will be okay, once he's dry?"

"I doubt it. He's a walking computer, full of electronics. Not a good mix with water. I should think his memory has been totally wiped. Have you spared a thought for your mum? What's she going to make of this? I don't know how I'm going to tell her."

"I'm sorry." And Tom really was, but the words sounded hollow even to his own ears and weren't enough to put this right. Nothing could. He turned and stared out through the rain-streaked window.

As soon as the car pulled up outside their house, the front door flew open and Mum came running down the short path.

"Stay here, Tom!" Dad said, getting out quickly.

Tom peered out through the rain at them. Dad was holding on to Mum's arm and she was looking up with an amused expression on her face. The rain started to come down harder, pelting off the windscreen and bonnet. Mum brushed Dad's arm away and came hurrying over to the car.

"What are you two up to?" she said, laughing, and then opened the back door with a flourish.

Boffin fell on to the tarmac at her feet.

"Aahh!" she screamed.

"Sshh!" Dad said. But the scream went on and on. He covered her mouth with his hand. "It's all right. There's nothing to be scared of. It's just a robot, like I told you. Please stop screaming, for all our sakes. We really don't want the neighbours noticing."

Mum nodded and swallowed hard. Dad took his hand away then bent down, lifted Boffin over his shoulder and carried him into the house.

Tom scrambled out of the car and went around to her. She was leaning back against it.

"You okay, Mum?"

"No! Of course not!" she snapped. The rain had turned her hair dark and drops were trickling off her fringe.

"I'm sorry," Tom said. He saw that she was shivering.

"Finn is . . . a robot?"

"Yes."

She covered her mouth with her hand and shook her head.

"We'd better go in, out of this rain," Tom said.

But Mum just stood, her eyes wide open, still shaking her head.

Dad was suddenly there, pushing past Tom.

"Come on, love," he said, taking her arm gently, helping her to the house and into an armchair.

Tom walked in after them.

"See what you've done," his dad turned on him. He waved his arm in Mum's direction. Tom saw how white she looked. "And look!" Dad pointed at Boffin who lay collapsed on the settee opposite.

"I'm sorry!" Tom shouted at the top of his voice. "I'm sorry, okay?"

"Oh, the poor thing!" Mum cried, sitting upright. "I can't bear to see him like that. Go get some towels, Tom! And my hairdryer."

Tom nodded. At last, someone was going to help. He ran up the stairs, two at a time.

When he came back down, he found Mum standing over Boffin. She'd taken his sweatshirt off. "To think, I had no idea. None at all. I wish you'd told us, Tom."

"I wish I had too." He held out a large bath towel. "Then this wouldn't have happened. But I was going to send him back to the museum tomorrow."

"I don't know how you got into this or what you were thinking of, Tom, but it was wrong! And you lied to us. All those lies! You left me worrying about his parents. How could you, Tom? How could you care so little for us?"

Mum snatched the towel away and turned her back on him while she dried Boffin's chest and arms. She gently wiped his face.

"He looked so real," she sighed. "And all that time he wasn't. Just a robot from the museum. And, oh, school! You took him to school! What will they think? You're going to be in such trouble."

Tom felt a sharp lump in his throat, one that he couldn't swallow. The pain seemed to spread to his upper chest.

"I don't care about school," he said quietly. "Boffin's ruined! And it's all my fault. Why did I take him to the pool?" He leant forward and opened Boffin's chest compartment, expecting water to gush out, but it didn't.

"Close it!" Mum shivered. "Ugh! That gives me the creeps. It's so unnatural. Pass me the hairdryer." She plugged it in and swept the nozzle backwards and forwards over Boffin.

"Where's Dad gone?" Tom asked, suddenly noticing that he wasn't in the room anymore.

"I'm here," his father spoke from the doorway, a phone in his hand.

"Don't phone them yet," said Mum. "Let me try and fix him first."

"Too late. I've spoken to the museum." He was quiet for a moment. Tom thought he looked grey. "And the police are on their way."

"The police!" Mum cried.

"But I didn't steal him! Dad, you've got to believe me!" Tom pleaded.

"Just now Tom, I don't know what to think. But whatever happens, you are our son, we'll be here for you."

Chapter Fourteen

Tom knew as soon as they arrived. A blue light flickered eerily about the living room. He felt like running, but that wouldn't be right and wouldn't be fair on Mum and Dad. He was the one the police wanted.

Dad went to the window and looked out. "A bit unnecessary," he said. "At least they didn't arrive with their sirens blaring. We're hardly going to do a runner with the robot now! Not after phoning and letting them know we had it. I'll go and let them in."

Tom glanced at his mum. She looked as scared as he felt – just standing there, wide-eyed, with her hands clasped in front of her. She bent to straighten Boffin's hat on his head.

"He looks okay, Mum. Leave him."

"They're in there," he heard Dad say.

The living room door swung open and in walked a lady police officer. She was closely followed by a much taller man. They were in full uniform, with peaked hats pulled down below eyebrow height. It made them look very stern.

The policewoman spoke first. "We understand," she said, "that you are in possession of a robot, a robot which was reported missing from the Science Museum on Thursday, last. Is that correct?"

"Yes," said Tom. "He's over there! But I didn't steal him."

The policewoman held up her hand to silence him. The other officer bent over the robot to have a look. "Yes, that's Boffin Brainchild all right. He's very lifelike!"

"Not without his clothes," Mum said.

"Ahem," said the policewoman.

Mum blushed and wiped some invisible dirt off her jeans.

"Perhaps we should all sit down." The policewoman pointed Tom to the settee and motioned Mum and Dad to chairs at the opposite end of the room.

They sat, waiting, as the policewoman spoke into a portable radio clipped to her jacket.

All Tom could hear at first was crackles and hisses – he couldn't make out anything that was being said. Then he caught a bit of their house address and heard Boffin Brainchild mentioned. The rest seemed to be in code numbers or something. Suddenly the woman officer was looking at him, unblinkingly. Her blue eyes had no warmth in them. "My name is Sergeant Sanchez. What's your name?"

"Tom."

"Tom. We have to ask you a few questions and Police Constable Matthews will write down your answers. Do you understand?"

"Yes." Tom shifted nervously on the settee.

"Before we begin I have to give you this caution. You do not have to say anything. However, it may harm your defence if you do not mention when questioned something which you later rely on in court. Anything you do say may be given in evidence. Do you understand?"

Tom looked nervously at Dad. Dad raised his eyebrows and nodded to go on.

To begin with the questions were easy. Then they got harder. Then they got annoying. She asked the same things over and over again.

"How did you get the robot out of the museum?" And, "Did anyone help you?"

Tom told them how Boffin had latched on to him,

how he had disabled the security cameras and then followed him on to the bus. They didn't seem to believe
him. They asked him again and again, until he shouted
at them.

"Why don't you
believe me?"

"I think he's had
enough now!" Dad
said.

You've surely got enough information. Can't the rest
wait until tomorrow?"

The officers looked at each other. PC Matthews
checked his watch and then scribbled another note.
Finally he closed his pad.

"Right, that will do for now," said Sergeant Sanchez.
"We'll take the robot with us. Fetch the box!" she said
to PC Matthews.

"You can't put him in there!" cried Tom when the
officer came back in. "It isn't big enough."

But PC Matthews ignored him, picked Boffin up and lowered him feet first into a square brown box. With only half of the robot in, he had to double Boffin over and squash him down, head first. Then the lid was sealed shut with a strip of parcel tape.

Tom followed them outside to the squad car and watched as they put the box into the boot. Banging it closed, Sergeant Sanchez turned to Dad.

"We'll give you a call tomorrow and let you know what the next steps will be. It might be a good idea to have a word with a solicitor."

Tom felt Dad's hand rest firmly on his shoulder. They stood in silence, side by side, and watched as the police turned their car in the quiet cul-de-sac and drove away.

Dad let out a long sigh. "We'd better go in so poor Mrs Tyson can get back to her sewing. She's there at her window. Give her a wave, Tom."

They both did.

"Mum or I will have to go around and tell her all about it later, I suppose. Don't feel like it now though." Dad hurried up the path.

A movement under the hedge caught Tom's attention. He saw a pair of feet with trainers on. They moved suddenly, then were out in the open.

"Jack! What are you doing here?"

"I didn't mean for it to happen. Honest! Is he . . . dead? You didn't tell them it was me, did you?"

"No."

"Really?"

"Go away, Jack!"

"Don't squeal on me, Tom. I'll do anything you want, but don't tell!"

"Get lost!"

Jack turned and ran, nearly tripping over the kerb at the corner.

Tom went inside. Boffin's hat was on the carpet in the living room. It must have fallen off when PC Matthews put him in the box. Tom picked it up and went upstairs. He needed to be alone for a few minutes. But his bedroom was full of all the stuff he and Boffin had done together. There were pages of their comic scattered all over the floor.

He folded up Boffin's bed and carried it back to the guest room, then picked up the drawings from the floor and put them away in his cupboard. Boffin's pyjamas lay neatly folded on a chair. Tom rolled them up and stuffed them into the black bin bag. That, too, went to the back of the wardrobe in the guest room.

There, Tom thought as he walked into his bedroom, *back to normal.*

He was sitting on the edge of his bed when Mum came in with a glass of orange juice and a biscuit.

"Thanks," he said, taking them. She didn't say anything, just patted his shoulder before going out again.

The late evening sunlight glinted off the orangey liquid in the glass. Tom remembered Boffin's orange tears rolling down each cheek. *All he wanted was to be like a real boy. Now he's just a pile of junk in a box.*

Chapter Fifteen

It was Sunday morning. Tom heard Mum and Dad tiptoe quietly past his bedroom and down the stairs. He rolled over in bed, turning his back on the door.

A distant *burr, burr* sound filtered up through the floorboards – someone was ringing the kitchen phone. He lay still, trying not to breathe so he could hear what was being said.

Seconds later he heard the rapid thumping of feet up the stairs and Dad burst into the room.

"You've got to get up, Tom. Come have some breakfast."

"I'm not hungry."

Dad, frowning deeply, came and sat on the edge of Tom's bed. "That was the police on the phone. They'll be here in an hour."

Tom pulled a face.

"I know, it's not what any of us wants this morning and we hoped you'd sleep on. But the police asked if they could bring the scientist who designed Boffin."

"Why?" Tom sat up.

"He needs to find out what Boffin did while he was here. It's important to his experiment, apparently. I wasn't sure whether to agree or not, but the police seemed to think it might help your position."

"I don't want to see him. I'm sorry for not telling you and Mum. I'm sorry for everything, okay? But Boffin's ruined. There's nothing I can do to make it better now."

"Please," said Dad. "Let's just co-operate for now. We can't be any worse off for meeting the man. Let's show willing, okay?"

"Okay," Tom sighed.

Dad paused in the doorway. "Perhaps, when you're dressed, you could go and say a cheery 'morning' to Mum. She's out in the garden."

* * *

"Hi, Mum," Tom said, as he stepped on to the garden path.

She was doubled over, picking up the remains of dead flower heads and putting them into a bucket. "Oh, good morning, dear." She flashed him a bright and breezy smile, but he knew it wasn't real. "I was just thinking about the first moment I saw Boffin," she said. "Why did he pull all the flowers off?"

"He was trying to smell them."

"And could he?"

"No."

"Of course not, silly me," said Mum. "He would need to have a sense of smell. And that would be impossible."

"He could feel the grass with his feet."

"Could he?"

"Yeah, he had tiny sensors on the soles of each foot."

"He was remarkable." Mum reached out to point at the dead flower heads that Boffin had taped back on. "I only noticed them this morning," she smiled sadly.

Tom smiled too. "He came down in the middle of the night to fix them for you. He really was sorry. And sad, when I told him he couldn't fix them, that they were dead."

"Oh, Tom! It's strange, but I feel like we've just lost a family member. I'm being ridiculous, aren't I?"

"No, you're not. I feel like that too."

"That's enough moping." Dad's deep voice startled them. "There's a plateful of hot, delicious pancakes in the kitchen, and they're ready to drizzle with lots of sticky syrup. You two had better come in before I finish the lot."

Tom tried to eat. Normally he loved pancakes and he and Dad always fought about who got the last one, but today he kept swallowing big chunks, which he'd hardly chewed, let alone tasted. He kept looking at the kitchen clock and watching the second hand tick by.

They'd just cleared the plates away when the doorbell rang.

"I'll answer it."

"Are you sure, Tom?" asked Mum.

"Let him," said Dad.

On the doorstep stood the same two police as yesterday, but in between them was a small, balding man. Tom smiled.

Now I know why you were mean, and didn't give Boffin hair.

"Good morning, Tom," said the policewoman. "This is Ishi Kashikoi, the man who invented Boffin Brainchild. He would like to ask you some questions. Is that all right?"

Tom nodded and showed them into the living room. Mum and Dad were waiting and came forward to shake hands.

Ishi Kashikoi looked uncomfortable with the contact, withdrawing his hand quickly from Dad's and sitting down.

Tom looked at him. The doctor stared back with cold grey eyes from a pale grey face. Even his suit was an insipid grey colour. Everyone seemed to wait for someone else to start the talking and finally they all did at once.

"No, you go ahead, Mr Kashikoi," Mum smiled.

"My name is 'Ishi' Kashikoi," he replied firmly, but

his eyes never left Tom's face. "Do you realise what you have done?"

Tom held his gaze. "Yes, and I'm sorry."

"The police tell me that Boffin wanted to go home with you. That he chose to. I find this hard to believe. Boffin would have had to develop complicated feelings. 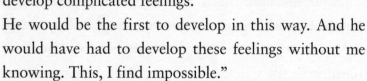 He would be the first to develop in this way. And he would have had to develop these feelings without me knowing. This, I find impossible."

"I've told the police," said Tom, "exactly what happened. I didn't steal your robot, he ran away from the museum because he was bored with it."

The doctor's paper-thin lips stretched fleetingly. "I would like you to take me through everything that happened. Every, little, detail."

"I've told the police. They wrote it all down."

The grey eyes narrowed. "I have every right to be extremely angry with you, young man . . ."

Dad stood up. So did the very tall Police Constable Matthews. Dad sat down. "Go on Tom," he said.

"But it will take all day."

"And is that too much to ask of you? You, who have interfered in my life's work, in one of the most important scientific experiments this decade, probably ruined a very valuable robot – and you find it hard to give me some of your time in order to tell me how Boffin spent his last few hours with you!"

Tom saw the urgency in Ishi Kashikoi's tightly controlled face. This was important. The man really needed to know. So he began from the first moment he saw Boffin in the museum. When lunchtime came Mum phoned for a takeaway. They stayed in the living room eating it. The police perched on the edge of the settee and everyone gathered close to hear as Tom continued with the whole adventure. Mum interrupted by asking if anyone wanted drinks. There were nods, but then no one touched the glasses she brought in. They were too intent on hearing about Boffin's day at school and to Tom's surprise Sergeant Sanchez laughed when she heard about the hair-cutting incident. Finally, Ishi Kashikoi stood up.

"Please will you show me around your home and your bedroom, where the toy robots are?"

"Okay." Tom got up and took the unsmiling man upstairs.

Ishi Kashikoi insisted on seeing the comics in Tom's bedside cupboard.

"Are all the pictures that Boffin drew here?" he asked. "These are everything that you and Boffin did together?"

"Yes."

And that's when it came to Tom. The pages in Ishi's hands were all the proof that he needed, because he and Boffin had used how they'd met as the basis for the first comic strip. He had proof!

"Look!" Tom said. "See, all I told you is true."

Ishi looked carefully at the drawings. "It's a good story. It doesn't make what you said true, they just show what a vivid imagination you've got."

"Boffin drew those, not me!"

"I know Boffin Brainchild has good drawing skills, but this," he waved the pages dismissively, "I find hard to accept. The story he tells is so full of emotion. Emotion! How did that develop? It would be . . . I can't tell you . . . if it was true!"

The police officers appeared behind them, making Tom jump.

"I think that is enough for the boy now," Sergeant Sanchez said.

"Thank you." Ishi Kashikoi bowed his head.

Tom held out his hand for the comics. The doctor clasped them to his chest. "No. I'll take these."

"But . . ."

"They are an important part of the Boffin Brainchild experiment. My property!"

There were no smiles, no further polite gestures, as he and the police left the room. Tom felt like banging the door closed after them, but he didn't. He sank back on the edge of his bed as he heard them leaving downstairs. Finally the front door closed and the car pulled away.

They still wouldn't believe him. They still thought he had stolen Boffin. Tom didn't know what was going to happen. They'd be back. And next time would they take him away and lock him up? Right now, he didn't care. All he could think of was that Ishi Kashikoi had taken the comics and he had nothing of Boffin left.

Chapter Sixteen

"Wake up! The police are downstairs."

"What?" Tom tried to open his eyes against the harsh glare of his bedroom light. Mum was bending over him and gently shaking his shoulder.

Suddenly, Dad was in the room too. "I'm going to put my foot down. They can't do this. Not in the middle of the night!"

"Do what?" Tom levered himself up on one elbow.

"The police have turned up, just like that, bang in the middle of the night and want to take you up to London."

"What will the neighbours think?" said Mum.

"I don't care about the neighbours. It's Tom I'm worried about."

"Don't you think I am too?" Mum wrung her hands.

"I'm sorry pet, let's not get upset. It's not like they're arresting him. At least I don't think so."

Tom felt himself go cold. He must have paled, because Dad said, "That was silly of me. Of course they're not going to arrest you. All that's happening is that the police want to take you up to London to see Ishi Kashi-koi. Okay?"

"But why can't it wait until the morning?" Mum asked.

Dad shrugged his shoulders.

"Well, there's no way," Mum pulled herself up straight, "I'm letting them take you up there on your own. Not to that weird little man!"

"He's not too bad," Dad said. "He could've been a lot worse."

"I didn't like him. I don't trust him."

"I don't know what to make of it all. So far, the man hasn't brought any charges against Tom. And he could have. Oh, I don't know, maybe we should do what they want for now. That all right with you, Tom? We'll be right there with you."

Tom nodded. He didn't feel like he had a choice.

Sergeant Sanchez and PC Matthews were waiting by their car. PC Matthews opened the back door and Tom felt like a criminal as they helped him in. He slid over to make room for Mum and Dad. They sat silently as the car gobbled up the empty motorway ahead. By the time they arrived in London, at a low single storey building, the sun was climbing into the sky.

They got out of the car. Tom shivered in the cool

early morning air. He had to clench his teeth to stop them from chattering together. Sergeant Sanchez guided him over to a large smoked glass door and pressed an intercom button on the wall. A security camera whirred overhead and Tom looked up at it. A crackly voice came through on the intercom. "Come in!" With a buzz the door swung  inwards. Ishi Kashikoi, his white lab coat billowing out, swooped on Tom.

"At last!" he said, catching hold of Tom's sleeve and dragging him away.

"Just a minute!" Tom heard his mum cry. "Wait for us!" But Ishi Kashikoi took no notice. Keeping a firm grip on Tom's wrist, he tugged him down a long corridor.

Plain white walls swept past as they rushed along endless grey mottled floor tiles. The place felt like a hospital. They stopped by a white door. Ishi Kashikoi shouldered it open. The spring-hinged door closed itself behind them with an eerie sigh and the doctor let go of Tom's wrist.

The room, sparsely furnished, had a wood-effect desk in the middle and on it stood a plastic robotic hand, wired up to a laptop. Tom looked around at the bare, stark white walls. One of them had a steel door in it. There were no pictures, except for a single glass mirror on which someone had scrawled a childish drawing of a robot, and some mathematical calculations.

"Say something to him! Anything! Just get him to come out now!" Ishi Kashikoi pointed at the steel door. "We must get him to open the door before his battery goes flat. And that could happen at any minute. For security reasons, the mini-lab has only one lock and that is on the inside. If he doesn't co-operate and open the door, we'll have no other choice but to use mini-explosives. And that might really be the end of him."

"The end of who?" asked Tom.

"Boffin, of course!"

"Boffin? Have you fixed him?"

"There was nothing wrong with him."

"But the water?"

"Boffin Brainchild was designed to be waterproof. He is able to be fully submerged."

"But he wouldn't talk or move . . . do anything."

"That's because you didn't recharge his battery

properly. The extra demands that the boosters needed for insulated mode sent him into temporary hibernation."

"You mean his battery was flat? That was all that was wrong with him? And all we needed to fix him was to plug him in?"

"Yes, yes, yes. Concentrate on now please. You must help me to get him out. He's in there, in my mini-lab. Everything to do with this experiment is locked in there with him. Everything! He could ruin it all. He went crazy. I've never seen him like that. As soon as we recharged him and he opened his eyes, he became . . ." Ishi Kashikoi paused, ". . . emotional. He kept asking for you. I couldn't do a thing with him and then when I went to get help, he locked me out."

"Boffin!" Tom called through the door. "It's me!"

"Tom!" came a tinny voice through the thick steel. "Why did you send me back here?"

Tom leant his head against the door. He didn't know what to say.

"Enough! Open this door, Boffin Brainchild!" shouted Ishi Kashikoi. "Now!"

"No!"

"Do as you are ordered. You're programmed to obey me!"

Tom turned and glared at the doctor. "Is that the way

you talk to him? No wonder he left. You can't talk to him like that. He's a very clever robot."

"Yes, you tell Ishi. Boffin Brainchild knows what he wants and that's to go home with Tom. I don't want to stay in lab, or go and stand all day in a museum. Boring! I want to live like a real boy."

The doctor pushed Tom to one side. "Come out and see Tom and we'll discuss this further."

"I want to talk to Tom, only Tom. Ishi must go away."

Ishi's face reddened. It was the first time Tom had seen any colour in it. "Okay, I'll leave you alone."

"Come out!" said Tom, once Ishi had left the room. "I want to make sure you're all right."

"Boffin half left."

Tom smiled. "Come on, Boffin. Ishi's gone now. Open the door!"

There was a clicking sound and then a loud clank. The steel door swung open.

"See," said Boffin. "They took my clothes away. I don't look like Tom now."

"Doesn't matter, you look okay to me."

"Why did you get rid of me?"

"I didn't. They came and took you away. Do you remember what happened? Jack pushing you into the pool?"

"Yes."

"I thought you were ruined."

"Ruined?"

"It means broken – that no one can fix you. I didn't know that you were able to go underwater."

"Yes, Boffin Brainchild fully submersible. I can't swim yet. I would like to learn. I would like you to teach me. Take me home now, Tom."

"I can't."

"Please."

"It's not that I don't want to. Believe me. I liked having you to stay and I miss having you around the place. You were fun."

"Tom getting mushy. Boys . . ."

"Don't get mushy. I know."

"Boffin wants to go home now!"

"Ishi Kashikoi won't let you. He needs you here. You're a very important experiment."

"I don't want to stay. I hate being a lab robot."

Tom coughed to clear his throat. "You belong here."

Boffin shook his head.

"Please, Boffin, don't make this hard for me. I don't like it either, but you've got to be good for the doctor. I'll write to you and send you comics, one every week. Maybe, if Ishi lets us, we could talk on the phone and maybe he might even let me come and visit."

"You want to visit me?"

"Of course I do. But Ishi won't let me if he thinks you're going to throw a wobbly every time I'm near. So you have to be good for him."

Boffin gave a small smile. His eyes blinked and he said, "Okay."

There was a noise behind them. Tom turned and saw Ishi Kashikoi with two overalled men in the doorway. He saw Ishi hold something out – like a TV remote control. Boffin must have seen it too, because he tried to hide behind Tom, but never made it. Suddenly he froze. His upper body collapsed forward so that his head reached his knees. For a moment his arms swung from side to side, then stilled. He looked like a dis-carded puppet.

"What have you done to him?" shouted Tom. "He was going to be good. I'd persuaded him. Turn him back on!"

"He was out of control." Ishi Kashikoi came into the room. "I need to re-programme him."

"He's fine as he is!"

"No, he must learn to do as I tell him. Put him away!" Ishi ordered the men.

They picked Boffin up and carried him into the mini-lab. There, they lay him on a metal table.

"You can't do this to him. You made the world's first free-thinking robot and then, because you don't like what he's thinking and what he wants to do, you switch him off. That's rubbish. You're rubbish. It's a lie! He's not free-thinking at all. You won't let him be."

"You're a boy. You don't know what you're talking about. It's time for you to go. Thank you for your help. I will make sure the charges against you are dropped."

"If I'd known you were going to do that to him, I wouldn't have helped you. I wouldn't have helped you for anything. I think you're being stupid. Stupid!" Tom shouted at him.

"People have invested a lot of money in this project. I can't let Boffin run wild when he feels like it."

"He wasn't running wild. He was learning lots. You didn't even know he could do half the stuff he was able to. Let him stay with us," Tom pleaded. "We'll look after him. You can keep an eye on what he's doing."

"Don't be absurd, little boy."

"I'm not a little boy. You don't care about Boffin at all, do you?"

Tom was so cross he was shaking. He'd never been so sure that a grown-up was wrong. He felt like hitting Ishi Kashi-koi. One of the overalled men must have sensed it, because he stepped forward and placed his hands gently on Tom's shoulders. "That's no way to talk to the doctor."

Tom felt outnumbered. There were three of them. There was nothing he could do for Boffin and nothing he said made any difference. He shrugged off the man's hands, sent Ishi Kashikoi a look of disgust and stormed out of the room. He tried to bang the door, but the spring-hinge wouldn't let him.

"What happened?" Mum and Dad asked him, when he'd finally managed to find them. They were sitting with the police in the reception area. Tom couldn't answer.

"What happened?" Dad asked again on the journey home.

But Tom was too upset to speak. He saw Mum and Dad exchange anxious glances, but he still couldn't form any words to explain. He felt too angry at the unfairness of it all and, worst of all, he knew that he'd helped to destroy Boffin.

Chapter Seventeen

On Tuesday, Tom went back to school. Sitting behind Sasha, he noticed that the ends of her hair had been cut even, to just below her shoulders. All day, Jack was like an eager-to-please puppy. He bounced up every time Tom needed something and fetched it. After lunch, Tom found bars of chocolate and packets of crisps on his chair. When he looked up, Jack gave him a creepy lop-sided smile.

"Where's Finn?" Mr Richardson asked.

Tom heard Jack's sharp intake of breath.

"At the doctor's," he replied, pleased at not having to fib. But an image came into his mind of Ishi Kashikoi standing over Boffin with a screwdriver, re-programming him.

"Tell him that I hope he's better soon," Sasha said over her shoulder.

Tom nodded.

It felt like a long day at school and, walking home afterwards, he found that he wasn't looking forward to the evening either. As soon as he got in and latched the front door behind him, Dad called, "Hello, Tom," from the kitchen. "I'm cooking my Bella Pasta."

Tom hung up his jacket and went through to the kitchen. Dad was alone. There was no sign of Mum. Then he heard the vacuum cleaner thumping about upstairs.

"Had a good day?"

"Okay-ish."

"Get me some tomatoes from the fridge, will you?"

Tom had his hands full when the doorbell rang. The noise from the vacuum cleaner stopped. Mum shouted down. "Is Tom home yet?"

"Yeah, I'm here."

"Get the door, will you?"

"Do I have to?"

"Don't be lazy, go on!" said Dad, rinsing his hands under the tap.

"Okay, if I have to." He dropped the tomatoes on the table and went through to the hall. The doorbell rang again, incessantly. Someone was holding the button down.

"I'm coming!" Tom shouted, fumbling with the catch. The loud buzzing was hurting his eardrums. He flung the door open.

"Boffin!"

"Hello, Tom."

"What are you doing here?" Tom grabbed hold of his arm and pulled him in. "Quick, before someone sees you." He slammed the door. "In here!" Tom pointed to the living room.

He rushed forward to close the kitchen door, before his parents saw him. It swung inwards, banging him in the face.

"Dad! Ahh!" He grasped his nose.

"Oh, hello, Boffin," said Dad and walked out again.

Tom stood for a moment, still holding his nose. He looked at Boffin, shook his head in disbelief, then walked after Dad.

"What do you mean, 'Oh, hello, Boffin'?"

Before Dad could answer, the doorbell went again.

"Get that, Tom!" said Dad.

"Can't you? I need to talk to Boffin."

"Tom," Dad said firmly. "Door!"

"Okay!"

"Hello," said Ishi Kashikoi. "I've—"

Tom closed the door in his face.

"That's no way to treat a visitor." Mum came running down the stairs, brushed past him and reopened it. "Come in, Mr Kashikoi."

"Ishi Kashikoi," he corrected her.

Tom backed into the living room. Boffin was sitting

180

on the settee. He was about to tell him to hide, but all he got out was "Hi—" when the doctor walked in, followed closely by Mum.

"Here are your clothes, Boffin," said Ishi Kashikoi, holding out a black suitcase. "I think you have everything you need in there."

"Thank you," said Boffin, beginning to bounce up and down on the settee.

Boing, boing, he went, getting higher and higher with every bounce. Tom's eyes followed him.

"Now remember," said Ishi Kashikoi, "you have to behave yourself or I'll take you straight back."

Boffin stopped immediately and sucked in his lips.

"What's going on here?" Tom looked from one of his parents to the other.

"Boffin has come to stay with us for a while," Mum said. "If that's okay with you? Ishi rang us this morning, when you were at school."

The doctor stretched his lips over his teeth in a slim smile. "Ishi Kashikoi, that's my name."

Mum blushed.

The doctor turned to Tom. "I am the world's leading robotics engineer. I have studied at the best universities. It has taken me years to gain the knowledge that I have. Your government is interested in this experiment. I have very rarely had my work or intentions doubted. You on the other hand, a mere schoolboy, dared to question my judgement."

"Yes." Tom held Ishi's gaze. "I thought you were wrong."

"I know you did. And though it pains me to have to admit it, I now agree with you."

"You do?"

"Yes. When I stopped thinking about my own importance and started thinking about the importance of Boffin and his future potential and well-being, it became obvious what was right. He learnt far more when he was in a normal family environment than he ever did in the lab. I have spoken to my partners and we feel it is within all our interests if Boffin can continue on his steep learning curve – with you. We feel that the progress he made with you was remarkable."

Boffin started bouncing again.

"You're happy about it, Tom?" Mum looked at him anxiously.

"Yes, but how long can he stay?"

"We're in talks about that," said Ishi Kashikoi.

"We've agreed to have him until the end of the summer," said Dad. "They have said he can even come camping with us."

The doctor took a black book out of his jacket pocket. "It would be very helpful if you could keep a diary, as well as keep me informed online. I have a brand new laptop for you in the car. Please record any important happenings, new experiences and so on. All information is valuable. Of course Boffin will have to visit the lab from time to time for us to check progress."

"Tom come too?" asked Boffin.

"Yes, if Tom wants to."

Boffin bounced higher. *Thump, thump, thump!*

"Do stop that, Boffin! Tom, I hope you know what you're letting yourself in for. He can be a handful sometimes." Ishi Kashikoi glared at Boffin.

"Just like a real boy," said Tom.

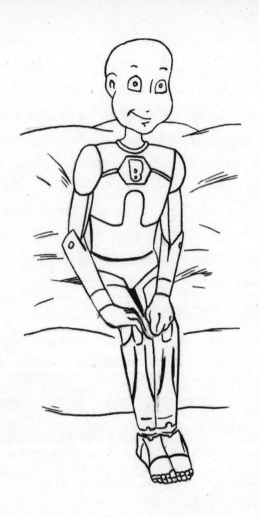